John Ferree

Autobiography of Prof. J.W. Ferree M.A.

Somewhat fragmentary and incoherent reminiscences written from memory

John Ferree

Autobiography of Prof. J.W. Ferree M.A.
Somewhat fragmentary and incoherent reminiscences written from memory

ISBN/EAN: 9783337124762

Printed in Europe, USA, Canada, Australia, Japan

Cover: Foto ©Raphael Reischuk / pixelio.de

More available books at **www.hansebooks.com**

AUTOBIOGRAPHY

of

PROF. J. W. FERREE M. A.

SOMEWHAT FRAGMENTARY AND INCOHERENT

REMINISCENCES

WRITTEN FROM MEMORY ALONE

WITHOUT ANY REFERENCES WHATEVER

TO A CHRONOLOGICAL DIARY

- 1892 -

PREFACE

Don't run! Hold a moment! My preface is brief.
Introduction short.

I have only to say that my sons have, for a long
time, importuned me to write my history. I declined yielding
to their request, because being a plain man, and having but a
meagre talent, and having accomplished but little of remarkable significance, I would have but little to record that would
be interesting. Besides having kept no Diary a thousand
incidents have faded from my recollection and vanished wholly
from my memory, many of which, perhaps, might be of some interest to record. I have however, finally surrendered my
opposition to their solicitations, and hasten to note or register
some scraps or sketches of my history of four score years. I am
not unconscious of it's imperfections. It may, however, rescue
from oblivion a few of the many incidents garnered in my memory.
Some of the incidents, perhaps, may be slightly varied for the
want of a clearer vision at this distance from them. The chief
threads of the narratives are reliable facts, however. If the
perusal affords the reader but little interest, let him, in some
degree attribute it to the intellect of the Biographer; the want
of written references; or a kept Diary detailing historic records.
The manuscript is not for publication, by any means, but only
 for the perusal of my own family. It is not broken into
customary chapters.   (This plan reversed.) J.W.F.

CHAPTER I

The ancestors of my maternal Grandfather, were of Brittish extraction or descent. They emigrated in about the year 1700 from the land of Erin, otherwise from "Sweet Ireland", the soil of the well known, witty Irishman. They braved the dangers of the deep, and found a home in the colony of New Jersey, and for some years resided there. The Fame of America lured them hither, where they were made welcome, making it permanently the land of their adoption. This first maternal, ancestral sojourner to our shores, was my Great Grand-Father, whose name was John Haslett, sometimes spelled Hazlett. His sons having arrived at manhood, left the Parental roof, and summoning courage and bravery, embarked to various destinations over the Colonies, where they could, if possible, improve their financial curcumstances. One of his sons, John Haslett, who afterwards became my Grand Father, repaired to Pennsylvania, exploring and threading his way to the Susquehannah River, and there settling, occupying lands on Chillisqua-que Creek, a small stream emptying into the Susquehannah River a few miles above Sunbury. Here, he married Miss Margaret Hood, a young lady, neat in her person; in her manners easy and affable; kind and gentle; with a good share of intellectual talent; and many a weary traveler in that early day found a restful home under her roof. Her character and life were without a spot or blemish. To them were born four sons and three daughters. The names of the sons were James, John, William and Samuel. The names of the daughters were Ann, Margaret and Jane. Samuel and Margaret were twins. They both attained the age of nearly "Three Score and Ten". Margaret was my mother. In about the year 1770 the Family removed about 80 miles N.W., and settled in the East end of Nittany Valley, three miles east of the present Village of Salona, and seven miles from the West Branch of the Susquehannah River.

Here he purchased several hundred acres of very excellent

the entire gentle, mountain slope to it's top. Chester County first
overs had owned all this part of the Colony. In it's division,
Northumberland County was formed in 1772. Again, in it's division
Center County was formed in 1800: and still later, Clinton County
in 1839.

The occupations of these four sons were as follows: James,
William and Samuel, farmers. John was a Teacher in the city of
Pittsburg. James for some years farmed his Father's Valley farm, and
about the year 1824 he removed to Venango County and purchased land
a few miles from the present City of Franklin, near Cooperstown on
Sugar Creek. William farmed on Bald Eagle Creek near the present city
of Lock Haven. He afterwards moved to Clearfield County and engaged
in the lumber business. Samuel in later years became a Preacher in
the Methodist Protestant Church. He also moved to Clearfield, and
located at Cherry Tree.

THE JOHN HASLETT FAMILY RECORD: HIS CHILDREN AND GRANDCHILDREN

John
Hasletts
children

My
Mother's
Father

James Haslett: lived in Venango Co., Pa. twice married
                                                    21 children
William Haslett: lived in Clearfiedl Co., Pa.   5   "

John Haslett: lived in Pittsburg, Pa.   4   "

Samuel Haslett: lived in Clearfiedl Co., Pa.   8   "

Ann Haslett: Married Rob't. Hurd, Center Co. Pa.5   "

Margaret Haslett: married Geo. Ferree, Center
                                    Co., Pa. 7 "

Jane Haslett: never married: lived in Center Co., Pa.

Ann died.
John lived in Franklin, Venango Co.,Pa. Dead.
William lives in Tionesta, Venango Co., Pa.
Clarissa married Mr. Shaw, Venango Co., Pa.
Sara Jane married Mr. Bowman, Coopertown, Venango Co., Pa.
Margaret married Rev. Beatty, Coopertown, Venango Co., Pa.
George lives at Tionesta, Venango Co., Pa.
James (called Jack) is a bachelor: lives everywhere.
Samuel is at Tionesta, Venango Co., Pa.
Peter Grove lives 2 miles from Cooperstown, Venango Co., Pa.
Julietta married Mr. Robison of Oil City, Venango Co., Pa.
Elizabeth married Mr. Herring of Cooperstown, Pa.
Rob't. lives near Cooperstown, Venango Co., Pa.

Stephen lives near Cooperstown, Venango Co., Pa.
Susanna married Mr. Thompson of Dempseytown, Venango Co., Pa.
Mary Lavina remained single near Cooperstown, Pa.
Rebecca married Mr. Hineman near Franklin, Pa.
Joseph lives at Dempseytown, Venango Co., Pa.
Benjamin lives near Cooperstown, Venango Co., Pa.
Hannah married Mr. Allison near Cooperstown, Pa.
Plummer is out West

Margaret married Nicolas McCracken,Bower, Clearfield Co., Pa.
Catharine married Arthur Bell, Bower, Clearfield Co., Pa.
John remained single
Elizabeth married David McCracken, Bower, Clearfield, Co.,Pa.
Sara married Templeton Haslett (her cousin), Cherry Tree, Pa.

June E. Ferree never married: lived in Mill Hall, Clinton Co.Pa.
J. W. Ferree married twice: Miss Frances Ann Herr & Diana J.Elliott
Harriet married Joseph Barrett, Prescott, Wisconsin
Joel & George (twins): Geo. died, 4 yrs. old: Joel lives in Minn.
Mary Ann died: 2 yrs. old. Salona, Clinton Co., Pa.
Christian N. died: 6 months and 10 days old

Maria married J. L. Churchill: Cherry Tree, Indiana Co., Pa.
Chamberlain went to Leo Kuk, Iowa   Co.
Templeton married Sarah Haslett (his cousin), Cherry Tree, Indiana
Samuel died: having married Miss Maria Ferron: Clearfield, Pa.
Greenwood: Clearfield Co., Pa.
Ann Eliza married William Armstrong: Cherry Tree, Indiana
Janus married William Dunkle: Clearfield Co., Pa.
Jane married Mr. Irvin: Clearfield Co., Pa.

John Wesley married in Salona, went West: died
Draper went West: died
Cynthia married John Wilmington: Mill Hall, both dead.
Sara married Rev. Henry Wilson: Salona, both dead

John P. Hurd married Mary Jane McGhee: Salona, Clinton Co., Pa.

Ann
Hurds
Children

Delinda married Peter Best: Freeport, Ill. or Cedarville, Ill.
William went West, near Freeport, Illinois.
Robert went West.
Margaret died at Salona, Clinton Co., Pa.

Jane never married, lived at Salona, Pa.

CHAPTER II

I may also add that James Haslett married a Miss Susannah Grove, who resided in the vicinity of Mill Hall. Grove Haslett, his son, who resides near Dempseytown, Venango Co., takes his mother's maiden name. James was twice married, his second wife being Miss Jane Hurd. John Haslett was married to a lady in Pittsburg where he was teaching.

William Haslett married Miss Elizabeth Wilson of Kittany Valley, near the present location of Salona. Salona was not then organized. It was organized in 1830, and named by the late Samuel Wilson, who was a brother of Elizabeth.

Samuel Haslett married a Miss Maria Ferron of Bald Eagle Creek, a few miles above Mill Hall, near Beech Creek. Ann Haslett married Robert Hurd, a farmer of Nittany Valley.

Margaret Haslett (my mother) married George Ferree, January 22, 1811. Jane Haslett never married. She remained in the home of her parents until their deaths. Grandfather resided on the mountain farm as it was called, in his well-constructed log house, until it was consumed by the flames. He then erected a fine stone building of solid masonry, in which he lived until his death. This farm, by his will, he gave to his youngest, single daughter, Jane. The Valley farm, by his will, was sold to George Brumoord for about $5000., and was equally divided among the six heirs. Jane lived for sometime in the old homestead, then sold the farm to Samuel Sigmund, a tailor in Salona for $1000. She then removed to Salona,

bought a property there, in which she lived for some years, then sold it
and afterwards made her home with her nephew, John P. Hurd until her
death. My Grandfather died in 1830, and was the first one buried in the
new Salona grave yard. Previous to this, all interments were made in the
further, east end of Nittany Valley on grounds of Samuel Furst, about one
mile east of grandfather's residence.

In 1821 my little brother, in his third year, and in 1822 my
little sister Mary Ann died in her first year. They were both buried among
the last in the old cemetery. So little did I understand the nature of
death, and the disposition of the body after it, that I was determined that
the man should not put my little brother in a box and bury him up in a
hold in the ground. I got the axe, and was about smashing the coffin,
but my parents prevented it.

My mother used to take me on the Sabbaths to visit their graves.
There she would remain weeping for hours. A mothers love for her
children is deep and unquencheable.

CHAPTER III

These historic sketches would be incomplete without some brief references made to the toils, burdens, and almost utter want of all the facilities for business and domestic relations of those primitive settlers. Prior to the year 1800, Nittany Valley was an almost unbroken forest, many miles in extent. The early inhabitants endured great privations and hardships. The settlements were distant from each other, and wholly devoid of the conveniences and comforts of modern times. The various improvements for facilitating agricultural labor, and abridging the servile drudgery of domestic life, were wholly unknown. Heavy burdens were their daily allotments, borne without any prospect of mitigation, until the struggle was released by completing the period of "three score years and ten". Their habitations were rude structures, quite insufficient to protect the inmates from the severity of the climate. They were also continually exposed to the peril of the wilderness, where the serpent hissed; the wild bird shrieked; the wolf howled; the panther screamed; and the hideous mid-night yells of the Indians broke the slumbers of the cabin, and the sleep of the cradle. They could not anticipate the day when the axe would wholly level their forests; when their cabins would vanish away; and on their ashes would spring up halls and residences of beauty and comfort. The axe, spade, shovel, and ill-formed plows were the only scanty implements that supplied the wants of the husbandman. The little cabin was both a kitchen and a parlor. Over the little domicile, the faithful wife with utensils as meager as those of her husband, presided, managing her domestic affairs with laudable frugality and economy. Their apparel found a wardrobe on nails driven in cabin logs. Their entire maintainance whether from field or cabin, was self-wrought, or home manufactured. To their eyes, the day was far in the distant future, when their condition would be made better, and they would emerge from the drudgery of forest life. Enduring incessant toils for daily sustenance, they coveted the

the night that brought them sweet repose. Their toils were preparations for the future comfort and hapiness of those who would follow. Long years, at last, brought them, one by one, a final rest from all their labors. No mournful sound of the tolling bell echoed through the solitudes of the forest announcing to the inmates of the little cabins in the neighborhood, that one of their tenants had gone. The plain funeral procession bore the departed away from the scenes of his labors to the place of his quiet repose. The spade and shovel soon veiled him from sight, and a long silence has closed over him. No chiseled monument, nor sculptured marble tells the spot of the quiet sleeper beneath. A rude stone told, for a little while, when he came, and when he went away, but it has long since refused to bear him record. Thus have the years, that wear away marble and granite, borne away all our ancestral worthies. "And no sound can awake them to glory again". The cemetery without any inclosure and attention; exposed to the resort and pasturage of cattle; was soon abandoned; and speedily laid waste. The willows have long since ceased to cast their shadows over the mounds that designated the spot of the remains beneath.

CHAPTER IV

I now leave this somewhat prolonged narrative of my maternal ancestry, and vary my pen to some references and historical sketches in the line of my Paternal ancestry, the lineage of the Ferree Family. The Ferree's were French of Huegunot descent. The Huegunots were French Protestants, renowned in Church History. For their christianity, thousands suffered martyrdom. Untold thousands more fled from France, their native country, to shun the reigning persecutions of the times. History records that about the year 1688, A.D., not less than five hundred thousand persons fled from France to other countries to save their lives. It is safe to say, that, during a few years about the above date, one million of those Puritan Huegunots left behind them their firesides, houses, lands, in

short, all their possessions, and fled with their children to other climes, to escape the fiery persecutions of the human fiends who held the supremacy of power, and whose delight it was to torture and slaughter the Protestants in all conceivalbe ways. Untold thousands suffered martyrdom, rather than renounce christianity, and blasheme that worthy name by which they were called. St. Paul, in his eleventh chapter of the Hebrews, well typed these horrible persecutions similar to those of his own day and prior. It would have been but justice, had a second Caesar, at a later day, scoured the land of the Gauls, and swept the murderous villains from the Continent, and like the devil with the swine, buried them in the sea. My Great, Great Grand Father, John Ferree, fell in these persecutions. He, in 1688, with nine others, was beheaded. The axe of the guillotine was raised and let fall, severing at one stroke, the heads of ten innocent victims. An extensive French record of the Ferree family is given in an old Bible, having the date of record 1688, A.D. This record states that John Ferree and Mary Ferree, his wife, were persons of rare endowments, of education, culture, and fortune. Because of their Protestant fidelity, social prominence and influence, the eyes of the persecuting demons were upon them. And having put the husband to death, they pursued the widow and her children, determined they should share the same fate. So to avoid detection, public exposure and death, she, for the time being, immediately changed her name, left her home and all her possessions, and, secretly, fled with her six children, three sons and three daughters, to Strasburg on the Rhine. For greater security, she soon left Strasburg and hastened to Linden in Germany. Not tarrying long, even here, she coursed her way onward to Holland. The sacred ties of family kindred, and the love of country being violently broken, she now resolved to leave France forever, the land of her nativity, and all of her possessions, and even the Old World itself, and make America her future, permanent home. She therefore left Holland for England, determined to take an early ship for the New

World. Upon arriving in England, she visited Queen Anne, wife of King
James, the second, and unbosomed her afflictions and sorrows to the Queen,
and sought the Queen's protection. For eight months refugees from
France, she and her children enjoyed the hospitalities of the Queen.
While a guest of the Royal Family she was introduced by the Queen to
William Penn. This noble personage of kind heart, took a great interest
in her welfare, deeply sympathizing with her in her persecutions and
losses. William Penn, learning that she was on her journey to America,
to make it her future home, determined she should settle in his Colony.
He insisted that she should take up her residence within it's limits.
He would accept no refusal. To induce her to accede to his request, he
presented or donated her, and each of her six children two thousand
acres of land. He gave her letters to his Agen, in Philadelphia,
authorizing him to locate Mary Ferree and her children on lands that he,
himself designated, and that are now ten miles from the present City of
Lancaster. The lands now embrace almost the entire Township of Paradise.
William Penn obtained his patent for this colony from the Brittish Crown
in 1681, in liquidation of a debt of sixteen thousand Pounds Sterling
($80,000) due his Father Admiral William Penn. King Charles was a
"little short" of money at the time, and in lieu thereof, gave William
Penn the territory of Pennsylvania, containing about thirty millions of
acres. This was at the rate of about four acres for a cent. The King's
signature was affixed to the charter, Mar. 4th, 1681 This charter
written on parchment, with the King's likeness on it, and all the lines
underscored with red ink; and it's borders gorgeously decorated with
various devices can now be seen among the archives of the State at
Harrisburg. The chartor vested the perpetual Proprietaryship of this
vast forest in Penn and his heirs on a fealty of the annual payment of
two beaver skins. William Penn thought he would call his Territory
New Wales, but afterward changed his mind, and thought that Sylvania

would be the most appropriate name for it, as it was covered with woods.
"The Latin word Sylva means woods). King Charles ordered that the word
Penn should be prefixed to the word Sylvania, in honor of Penn's Father.
To this Penn objected: he thought it would savor a little too much of
vanity. Penn offered the King's Secretary twenty guineas($100.) if he
would not prefix the word Penn, but the Secretary would not take the
money. In 1682 Penn embarked for his new Colony. He set his foot for
the first time in America, Oct. 24th of that year. He had peaceful
interviews with nineteen tribes of Indians, purchased and paid them for
their lands, and by his good will, justice, and kindness towards them,
secured the unbroken friendship of the Indians for seventy years, thus
preserving the land of Penn free from the scalping knife and tomahawk.

CHAPTER V

This famous treaty of William Penn with the Indians was made
the last day of November, 1682, under a large Elm Tree at Shackamaxon
(now Kensington) and now included within the present chartered limits of
Philadelphia. The Colony continued in the Penn Family until the
Revolution, when it was purchased by the State for $580,000. Mary Ferree
now (1688) began to make preparations to take shipping and embark for
New York. Queen Ann, very kindly, and gratuitously furnished her a
complete outfit of house furniture, and all the farming utensils necessary
for her new home, in the new Colony, in the new world. When she arrived
in New York, to her great surprise and delight, she hailed a number of
her relatives and friends from France, who had also fled from the
persecutions there, and were taking yp their permanent also in America.
She remained several days in New York, and then with several of her
relatives and friends, went to Philadelphia and presented her papers
of "Land Grants", which she had from William Penn to his Agent there.
The Agent and entire party now set out for the lands designated by
William Penn, and which was to be the future home of the first Ferree

Family in America. The lands lay in the Pequad Valley, so named from the tribe of Indians residing there. Their Village of wigwams stood where the beautiful town of Paradise now stands. (As stated above, Paradise is ten miles east of the present city of Lancaster) The Indians welcomed them with a warm reception. When the Indian Chief, who signed William Penn's illustrious treaty observed the whites manifesting some little timidity, he said to Mrs. Ferree, "Indian no hurt white: white good to Indian". The Chief with a magnanimity of humanity that would have done honor to a higher civilization and refinement, vacated his wigwam, and gave it up to Mary Ferree and her children permanently. They exchanged venison for bread and milk, and lived on most friendly terms without a fear ever afterwards. The first white child born within the limits of Lancaster County was a Ferree. Lancaster County was formed in 1729. Prior to that date it was included in Chester County. Penn divided his Colony into three counties: Viz, Philadelphia, Chester and Bucks.

The graveyard, a burial of that place and day (200 years ago), containing an acre of ground, has still it's substantial stone wall around it, as solid and compace as when it was first put up. The inscriptions of the Ferree Families and others out in the tombstones, preserving the memory of the deceased, are still distinctly and indeliby legible. The church built, and donated to the citizens by William Penn, still stands and is the Temple, at present occupied by Quaker worshippers. The house in which Penn himself lived, in Philadelphia, is still standing.

CHAPTER VI

Prior and subsequent to the year 1800, there arrived in this part of Nittany Valley a large number of settlers noble Families, relatives of each other from Lancaster City and County in this State. These eminent personages left their cultural homes, bidding adieu to ease and comfort, and, at that distant day, journied to afar off lands awaiting their cultivation. Their fine intellectual abilities; endowments; financial resources; untiring industry; amiableness and worth, made them a blessing to the Valley. When they arrived, times and prospects started on the advance. The wives were all sisters, descendents of a wealthy distinguished Family, (The Bresslers), who had previously purchased a large domain in this part of Center County, which County was then just organized. Clinton County, organized in 1839, now includes this part of Center County. To these heirs of George Bressler,Esq. of Lancaster County, was bequeathed a large landed estate, each one sharing in the property. The son and all the sisters were married. The son was the late Hon. George Bressler of Mill Hall. He came to Center County about the year 1812. The daughters names were as follows - Catharine, wife of Samuel Wilson, Elizabeth, wife of Jacob Hartman. Fanny, wife of Joel Herr. Mary (usually called Polly) wife of Joel Ferree, and Grand Mother of the writer. These four sisters came to Center County (at that time Northumberland County) in 1794. Northumberland County was organized in 1772, and Center County in 1800, as previously stated.Rebecca, wife of Daniel Herr, came to Center County in 1814. Her husband died suddenly in Columbia, Lancaster County, while on his way to Center Co. Just after he had deposited his goods in a Keel boat for shipment up the waters of the Susquehanna. At that early day, freight, and often passengers were transported in low flat-bottomed boats. The boats, or "flats" as they were called, were urged forward up the stream of river currents, by strong, vigorous men placing heavy poles against their shoulders, and

pushing with all their strength in single file on each side of the boat.
Harriet, wife of Samuel Miller, came to Center County in 1830, her
husband having previously died in Lancaster. Charlotte, wife of
Henry Barnett, remained in Lancaster City, her husband having also died.
She made frequent visits to Center and Clinton Counties, visiting
relatives, but never permanently residing there. They gave symmetry,
complexion, and direction to this part of Nittany Valley. They all
attained an unusual longevity; their mother reaching the age of 107 years.
Because of their protracted lives, they were very properly and fitly
styled the "Old Aunts" by the relatives and citizens of Salona and the
Valley. Their minds were well balanced. They had correct views of
subjects. Hence, they were seldom deceived, or mislead in the affairs
of life. They were not victims of imposing credulity. Their credulity
was founded in the exercise of their naturally strong common sense in
the fitness of things. Their sound judgment reposed the tendency to put
full faith in conclusions, founded on insufficient data. They were
intimately versed in the scriptures; admired for their excellences;
enduring; patient; kind; highly respected and honored. No shadows
veiled their declining years. Their names are recorded as splendid
monuments in the history of the Valley. Their old age was serene and
delightful, like a beautiful evening sky without a cloud. At this writing, they have all quietly passed away. They were borne to their final
resting place in expressions of sorrow by a concourse of people, who
delighted to esteem their virtues; cherish their names, and revere their
memories. "Peace to their ashes".

My Paternal Grand Father had four brothers - John, Thomas,
Elisha and Ephraim. My Grand Father's name was Joel. He was a farmer,
John was a Saddler, Thomas kept a Hotel in Pittsburg. Elisha was a
Fuller, Ephraim was a Hatter. They were all born in Lancaster County.

CHAPTER VII

My Grand Father, Joel Ferree, who came from Lacanster, bought
between 200 and 400 acres of land in 1794 from Mr. Anderson where the
Village of Salona now stands and vicinity. He payed the sum of 416
pounds, 4 shillings, 6d, Sterling ≅ $2014.51 for it. He paid it in gold
and silver. The tract is called the "Deep Spring Farm". The house is
quite adjacent to the "Spring." It was built by my Grand Father. The
late Samuel Wilson resided in it. His widow (Elizabeth Wilson) still
lives in it. It has received additions at the ends, but the central
body of the house is the original structure. It is perhaps the oldest
house in the Valley, and is still a noble mansion, promising nicely to
shelter it's inmates for many years yet to come. * Strange to say, the
cedar posts, fencing the garden lot, are still in the ground, showing no
signs of decay, although they are 100 years. George Bresslet (son)
bought this farm from my Grand Father in 1801 for 845 pounds Sterling or
$4089.80 My Father, George Ferree was born in Strasburg, Lancaster Co.,Pa.,
Oct. 11th, 1786. He was clerk in a dry goods store in Lancaster City,
but his father's family, and a large number of his relatives (The
Bresslers, Hartman's, Herr's, and Wilson's) having removed to Nittany
Valley from Lancaster City and County, in 1794 he followed them to their
new homes. Here he became a skilful mill-wright, and indeed a most apt
masterpiece in erecting all other buildings. He was an ingenious
Architect in manufacturing all kinds of cabinet work, and making patterns
and mouldings of curious designs for castings. He was a very superior
mechanic and expert in all the devices of wood designs, giving beautiful
forms to all kinds of wood models. He also, as an artist, had a natural

* The Original House was torn down by the Silica Sand Co. of
  Montoursville, Pa., who purchased the house and the holdings
  in 1950.

aptitude for ornamental wood painting, beautifully imitating all the
varieties of wood. The veins, knots, curved lines, and grains in
mahogany, oak, maple, cherry etc., were delineated as richly and perfectly
as in the natural wood. His brush gave all the tints, veins, and
shadings of marble in such exquisitely beautiful imitations, so true to
nature, as scarcely to be distinguished from the polished, natural
marble itself.

Sometime subsequent to 1794, Henry Marsh of Lancaster, nephew
of Joel Ferree, took a trip on horseback (150 miles) through the wilderness or "back woods" as the central part of Pennsylvania was then called,
to visit his Uncle Joel. Joel then lived in the house he built, and
which now stands at the "Deep Spring". On his journey he sometimes
encamped out during the night, and heard the howling of wolves, and the
screams of the panther. Approaching the end of his journey, penetrating
the woods, and nearing the house of his Uncle, he heard soft, sweet
voice tones. Pausing a moment to catch the musical sounds, he, at once
recognized the voice of his Aunt "Polly" (Mary): my Paternal Grand Mother.
On his return, he told them, he had seen little else than woods, streams,
foxes, deer, bears, and panthers.

CHAPTER VIII

February 2nd, 1814 was my natal day. Auspicious day! Propitious
the star that presided over my natal hour. My eyes now, for the first
time, saw the light and I dawned into society, making my incipient appearance as a promising citizen of the Republic. The little log cabin, my
original infant home was about one mile west of the present Villiage of
Balona, in the vicinity of the late James Brown. The little domicile
stood near the foot of a hill, due north of Mr. Brown's residence, and but
a few rods from a little brook called Cedar Run. After a time it was
vacated, and left it's primitive location, it's honor, by busy hands,

being conveyed on snow and ice, a little further down the stream, tarrying at the confluence of the Run and Fishing Creek. Here it joined a company of similar cabins, and for some years profitably contributed it's Palatial - self and services in promoting the interests of a Tannery. It has long since finished it's work, and disappeared from the community, "having gone the way of all the earth". My Father removed from this place to about one mile below Mill Hall, (now Sandersons) and was there employed as a Mill Wright to put up a large flouring mill for his Uncle George Bressler (Jun). My mother here, attended to all her household duties, and boarded seventeen workmen besides.

The mill being completed, his Uncle requested my Father to run the mill, which, by experience, he was well qualified to do. This offer he accepted. No canals or raiil-roads being in those early days, the flour and grain were conveyed or transported to the city markets in large Arks, or open boats on the rivers in the spring floods. To have the barrels of superfine flour ready for the early spring floods, it was necessary to run the mill all night in the winter season. This Father could not do alone. He therefore employed a journeyman miller to assist him. They ran the mill together, taking alternately six hours each. Here a very fatal incident occurred. The journeyman in his turn in the night, it is supposed, laid down in the Office of the Mill and fell asleep. When the grain in the various hoppers was all ground, and the hoppers empty the (mill stones) would run with increased velocity, and by their friction would issue streams of sparks and fire, setting all the surrounding woodwork in a blaze. My Father awoke in the night, and seeing the mill on fire, hastened to rescue the journeyman and what he could, but the conflagration had proceeded so far, the whole interior being filled with smoke and flame, nothing could be saved. The journeyman was consumed in the flames. George Bressler afterwards rebuilt his mill, brought up a store, and established a large Furnace in Mill Hall.

CHAPTER IX

My Father now moved to Mill Hall and ran a mill for Nathan Harvey. It was an extensive Flouring Mill. I was now two years old, and have in memory several incidents retained from that early age. I will narrate them.1 - After heavy rains, muddy streams are great feasts for eels. Fishing Creek was but a few rods from our house, and abounded in these snake-fish. A heavy evening rain stirred them up lively in the creek. My Father, in the night, set his fishnet for them. In the morning he brought in a bucket full of live eels, and poured them all out in the middle of the floor. My mother screamed, as they crawled like snakes over the floor. (No carpet in those days.) This was an impressive exhibition for young eyes, and has never been forgotten. My Mother would never eat them: she said they looked too much like snakes. 2 - Another incident I remember. There was a very deep snow. My Father shovelled a path from the house to the mill. The walls of snow were so hight, that when I was in the path, I could not reach to the top or see over them. 3 - Another incident: In the winter season, I stood on a chair at the window, and a number of men with glittering knives in a pig pen, made them squeal terribly. I had great compassion for the pigs, and thought the men were very cruel. 4 - Still another incident. Nathan Harvey, whose mill Father was running, had a colored man living with him, whose name was "Mell". Mell was a very pure-minded man, innocent, honest, truthful; upright in his life; and was very highly respected in the community. Nathan Harvey was a man of high temper. In his fits of wrath and boiling anger, he would frequently take "Mell" into the barn and beat and thrash him with the horse whip, his screams being heard far away. My little ears, hearing his cries, I would run under the bed, and stop my ears with my fingers. It was a brutal outrage, and should have been suppressed by the community. It was a miracle that "Mell" still remained with him. He should have left him or returned the hiding.

This same man, Nathan Harvey, came very near meeting with a fatal doom. Having a love for money more than a love for Country, in the war of 1812, he shipped ark loads of flour down the West Branch of the Susquehanna River, and sold it at a high figure to the British, who then quartered in the vicinity of Baltimore. This was contrary to the Laws of Belligerent Nations - furnishing provisions to the enemy. Our Government learning this transaction, arrested Nathan, tried him by Military Laws, and assigned him to be hung. This news reaching the ears of his brother Samuel Harvey, a rich, influential Banker, and a local Methodist Preacher, who lived in Germantown, near Philadelphie, he hastened to Washington to rescue his brother, if possible, from his impending fate. In a conference with James Madison, who was then President of the United States, and also the head of the army, Samuel succeeded in redeeming his brother Nathan from his deserved execution, by paying down $20,000 for his neck. To indemnify his brother Samuel for his life, Nathan conveyed over to his brother Samuel, his mill, store and all his Mill Hall property, and was thus reduced to poverty. "The way of transgressors is hard". Bible.

The Furnace of George Bressler in Mill Hall and it's surroundings; the flames of fire streaming up out of the high chimneys by day and by night; the numerous teams with ponderous wagons behind them decamping in all directions, were great curiosities to my young eyes, and of great admiration.

One team of all others attracted my especial attention. It had no competition or rivalry. It was driven by a very large surly Irishman, whose name was Peter McCaslin. He was a complete masterpiece among horses. He drove six mammoth, Elephant Bays, each with almost the strength of an elephant. He had them under perfect discipline. He carried a massive whip, which he seldom, if ever, used. But when he rolled a peal from the end of the silk cracker, to my boyish ears,

it had the sound of a cannon explosion. When the majestic six heard it, they knew there was a necessity for it, that Peter meant business. It was the watch-word for onward. When he gave the gentle command to go forward, there was no prancing, nor dancing, nor balking, but a quick preparation to take the massive load of iron out of the deep, tough mud. Their feet were extended, their bellies crouched, and went down nearly to the ground. The harness chains were stretched to their utmost tension. The wagon creaked and grated, but the wheels were sure to turn. A failure in the movement would have been because every trace had snapped asunder. Nothing was said. The one original command was stereotyped, and meant motion not trial. That the 6 steeds understood as well as Peter.

Uncle Bressler (My Father's Uncle) some years afterwards did a thing unwittingly, much to his financial injury: but he did it in the best of faith. To aid him in his extensive work, he took in a man, as a partner, whose name was Henry Kinney. Kinney had no finances, and invested no capital in the concern. He, the scheming rascal, taking advantage of Uncle Bressler's great financial credit all over the country, secretly, without Uncle Bressler's knowledge, complotted the design of enriching himself through Uncle Bressler. To effect this, he borrowed untold thousands of dollars all over the country, and gave the parties judgment notes signed Bressler & Kinney. When he amassed a vast amount, he "fled the country". When it was noised abroad that Kinney, one of the firm, had left the country, the note-holders came in on Uncle Bressler like a flood, and swept his mill, store, farm, furnace, ore lands, and all his property, and reduced him to abject poverty.

CHAPTER X

Mohn McGhee, a merchant from Center Co. (or rather from Penns Valley), removed to the present site of Salona, and there established a store. He employed my Father to build him a Flouring Mill there. Hence,

my Father, moved from Mill Hall to put up the mill and lived in the
house now occupied by John P. hurd in Salona.

The mill was built, and has done a fine and extensive work.
It is a stone structure, and still remains in active operation. McGhee
became a very intimate friend of the bottle. It cost him many thousands
of dollars. He would often take Ark loads of Superfine Flour and an
immense amount of wheat to the cities on the spring floods, and would
come home after a month or two spreeing and merry frolicking, with not
a cent in his pocket. He died in 1831, leaving little property. Had he
been a temperate man, he might have left a respectable fortune. I was
now about 6 years old. My Aunt Jane Haslett would pay us frecuent visits.
She would devote much of her time in trying to quiet the young folks.
I had already acquired quite a reputation for being a , playfully,
noisy fellow. For these often offences Aunt Jane would imprison me in
the dark closet, which was by no means congenial to me. But fair
promises soon brought me a pleasant release, and I was ushered out into
daylight again. Here I commenced my educational history. Little did I,
then, fancy that it was the initial of my chief Professional Life. The
little school cabin was on a hill in the rear of the residence now
occupied by the widow (Catharine) of the late George Herr. Father made
a fine little snow sled with a box on it, for my sister Jane and myself. Jane was older than myself. He would put us in the box, and pull
us up to the College on the snow. My Library, which I, very carefully,
carried back and forth with me, consisted in a little blue primer of
two or three leaves, having three or four rows of variously, and curiously
shaped figures, called letters, on them. The rows seemed long distances
from the top to the bottom. Whether in that first winter, I got down
as far as where izzard lived, I am now quite unable to tell.

The presiding genius was David Logan. He was master, not
teacher. There were no Teachers in those days. He gave the young
divines to understand that he was "monarch" of the inclosure - "of all he
surveyed". He was commanding, rigid, and stern: schoolastic fears
alone allayed his wanted severities. We, little ones, used to sit mute
and breathless in the home chimney corners at night, under pine-knot
lights, and in fearful quiet timidity listen to him telling about a
terrible encounter he had in Bedford County with a panther. He was
riding on a horse through a lonely, desolate country, and evening settling down upon him, and darkness just as he entered a thick woods of
several miles in extent without a house. He had not proceeded far, until
he heard what seemed to him the cry of a child; yet he knew this was im-
possible. He, then, remembered the saying, that the scream of a panther
is very similiar to the voice of a child. He interpreted the scream as
being that only of a panther. Although the horse, all the while, was
under a fast momement, he heard a second scream nearer than the first. He
was now fully apprised that the animal was in pursuit of him, and gaining
on him. He became greatly alarmed. He put spurs to his horse, incit-
ing and urging him to the swiftest flight, knowing this was his only
safety. Strange to say, the panther did not follow the road in the track
of the horse, but kept in the woods. When the horse ran round curves
in the road, the panther ran in straight lines - the chord of the arc, and
was at the end of the curve ready to spring upon it's victim. It sprang
several times at him, but the horse going rapidly forward, the panther
sailed over behind him. Only once he threw out his claw and took a good
patch out of his flying coat shirt. Finally, emerging from the woods,
he reached a farm house on the road, when by the barking of the dogs, the
panther left him.

CHAPTER XI

In about the year 1820 a terrible tragedy occurred near Curvensville, Clearfield County, Pa., that greatly excited the whole Valley. It was the chief topic of conversation in all houses, far and near. I was then about six years old, very timid, fearful, and alarmed in hearing the many conversations of visitors at our house on this exciting topic. It was my usual fashion, when visitors came to our house, to run under the bed and hide, breathless, till they went away. But under the influence of this story, my best place of resort was to thrust my head under my mother's apron, as the place of greatest safety. Though then so young, but hearing the story so often, I could relate it about as well as I can tell it now. The recital is thus - Mr. Reuben Giles, a gentleman and citizen of New Jersey, set out on horseback to visit some relatives in the State of Ohio. He had a son living near Bloomsburg, Columbia Co., Pa., on the North Branch of the Susquehanna River. Mr. Giles, on his way, rested several days with his son, leaving his horse there to rest, and taking his son's horse instead. He continued his journey, but no word or account came from him afterwards. His family, at home, and his son became very uneasy and alarmed about him fearing something had befallen him, for several weeks had elapsed since he left. The son at Bloomsburg delayed no longer at home to hear from him, but departed in haste in pursuit of him. He traced him plainly and satisfactorily by day and by night in his arrivals, lodgings and departures, to Curvensville, a town on the Allegheny mountains in Center Co., Pa. He could now trace him no further. No distance near or remote beyond this, could reveal anything respecting him. Hence, the son entertained no doubt but that his Father had fallen into foul hands in those regions. He, therefore, summoned a party of men and searched the woods for miles on each side of the road. The son was satisfied that the outrage was committed on the road, because he left the town in the morning in safety.

But after frequent trailings and explorations in quest of him, it was of
no avail: he could not be found. The men, therefore, gave up the pursuit,
and were homeward bound. Pausing on the road at a farm fence, and lean-
ing on the bars, and a pasture near inclosing some horses, the son
remarked, "why there is my horse, Come here Tom", and the horse came running to him. The men went to the farm house, and asked the man where he
got that horse. He replied that he bought him out of a drove of horses.
The men said, there has been no drove of horses along here. The man
looked confused. The men saw on the man's shirt collar the name "Reuben
Giles". His name was Monks. He was now identified, plainly, as the
murderer. The men continued the search near his residence, and found the
murdered man. Monks was arrested, put in the Bellefonte jail, tried,
convicted, and sentenced to be hung. He confessed the murder. He said
he was out hunting and passed Giles on the road, and turned round and
shot him. Giles fell from his horse, and said to Monks, "My friend you
have shot me". Monks gave him several blows on the head with a hatchet,
and dragged him in the woods. Many people went up from the Valley to the
execution. He was hung out-doors.

CHAPTER XII

I may record here, that my Father had one brother and four
sisters. They all hailed from Lancaster at an early day, except the
younger sister Rebecca. She moved to Mill Hall in about 1836. They were
all married. Uncle Joel married Miss Jane Forgy of Dunnstown, a Village
opposite the City of Lock Haven. My Uncle was a very fine plasterer.
Some of his work remains to this day, in good condition, though nearly
one hundred years old. Polly, as she was called, the oldest sister,
married James Dunnahay. Charlotte, the second sister, married David Logan,
of whom I have spoken above in the panther celebrity. Eliza, the third
sister, married a Mr. Robison who died in Lancaster. She afterwards

married Isaac Ditsworth of Harrisburg, a superior plasterer, and a great
mechanical genius. Rebecca married Jacob Kauffman of Lancaster City,
who carried on an extensive business in the fresh meat market. He
employed a number of men, but he superintended only. These four husbands*
were all inclined, more or less, to the **bottle.** Indeed, in those early
days, few irreligious men could be found wholly exempt from the intoxicating libations. To find a Temperance man was an exception, not the rule.
Distilleries could be seen steaming in all directions, more plentiful
than school houses or churches. *Robinson excepted. The liquor habits
and consequent drunkeness were almost universally prevalent. Jacob
Kauffman, Rebecca's husband, was a kind, respectable, and excellent man
when he was sober, but he was excessively given to the intoxicants. And
when he was under it's influence, he was crazy, raving, and fiendish. He
would pursue his wife and children with a club, or butcher knife, with an
intent to kill. They would flee from him, and hide in rooms or closets,
or hasten to the neighbors for protection. He, daily, handled a large
amount of money. But when under the influence of whiskey, he would throw
it round everywhere, and when he became sober, he would never inquire anything about the money he had wasted. Aunt Rebecca seeing that, that kind
of life could not last long, and that she and her five children would soon
be reduced to poverty, she began secretly, without his knowledge, to
gather up the "roll of bills" that Jacob was scattering round broadcast
when he was drunk. Thus she wisely accumulated many thousands of dollars.
Jacob became so desperate and dangerous, that she began to entertain the
idea of obtaining a divorce, which the neighbors requested her to do.
She finally obtained a divorce from the Court, and removed, she and her
children to Mill Hall (then Center Co., now Clinton Co.) Here she
established a dry goods store, and also grocery. Jacob, sometime afterwards abandoned his drinking, and became a sober, temperate man. He
joined the Methodist church and remained a faithful member until his death.

Rebecca, in Mill Hall, had in the mean time, also joined the Methodist church. Jacob, in Ohio was cherishing the idea of Paying a visit to Rebecca and his children. He did so: and his arriving visit resulted in their re-marriage. They went to Ohio, and there remained until their death. He left considerable property to each of his children. In 1836 my uncle Joel Ferree, my Father's brother, removed to the State of Ill., Adams Co., in the vicinity of the City of Quincy.* After some years he died there, and to his widow and her two sisters was left a large fortune, in England, by their Uncle: a million in money. Ten years elapsed before it crossed the ocean. The multiplicity of hands through which it went, of Agents, Government Officials, letigations, etc. reduced the vast amount, so that each sister finally obtained but $1000., apiece. $997,000 were spent in obtaining it. Each sister should have received over $333,000. I believe this is about the outcome of most foreign fortunes. The scheming rascals, agents, I will rather say, thieves and robbers simmer down the mountains to molehills.

*Rev. S. G. Ferree, my cousin, is a son of Uncle Joel Ferree, and a member of the Illinois Conference.

CHAPTER XIII

My Father having completed the evection of the McGhee Flouring Mill, formerly alluded to, my Grandfather requested my Father to occupy one of his houses on the Valley farm near him, as my Father's occupation in Mill Wrighting called him away from home so much of his time. These lands, the Valley and mountain farm, were most excellent soils. In cereals (grains) and all agricultural products, they were among the richest in the State. Their culture yeilded ample rewards. Large orchards of apples and peaches were yearly on both farms, in plenitude and great variety. There was no yearly failure, when the fall season arrived, producing the maturity of fruits, apples and peaches, it was the custom of my Grand Father to summon the boys of the Valley for a week or two,

to gather the fruit of his orchards, and store them in his capacious
four horse wagone, to be conveyed away to his cider presses. This was
magnificent sport for the young urchins of the Valley. In those days
it was customary for every family in the Valley to make a barrel of apple-
butter for the winter. This made a great demand for apples and cider.
The apple-butter went on slices of bread in the boys and girls school
basket.

      My Grand Father Haslett being of Irish extraction, was naturally
a little, and inelegant in his conversation, sometimes. In his disposition and tongue he was not as smoothe and mellow as many others. He
had, without any intention, inherited a small degree of ugliness, on his
tongue, which might be styled dogsnaps: a little snarly, growly-like.
No suggestion was favorably received at first. He was sure to grunt
emphatic negatives to first propositions. When favors were first asked
of him, he declined the gift, but after a time, he would turn up a allright, modify his tone, disposition, sentiment, mellow and soften his
language; be as congenial as the best; and very pleasantly furnish any
gift in his power to bestow. No one ever left his house in want of any
charity or benefaction in his possession. He, unwisely, transmitted a
little of his moody aptitudes to his heirs. One little incident will be
sufficient to indicate his **bent**. When I was ten years old, my Father
sent me over to Grand Father's to get his team and hired-man to haul some
wood. I found him and his hired-man in the woods with the snow-sled hauling wood for himself. I made known my errand to him. He growled out
positively "No": we are hauling wood for ourselves." I loitered round a
minute or two, and left for home. I had got a little way off when he
looked up and saw me, and said, "Where are you going?" I said, I am
going home. "Going home" he snarled out: "without knowing whether you
can get the team or not." "Come, he said, and put these chips on the sled
and Jonathan will go over and haul your wood." His gruffness had sub-
sided and he had become **normal.**

CHAPTER XIV

Here I entered upon my first financial career. My vocation consisted in catching rats. My Grand Father's barn in the Valley, near our house, was infested with these repulsive animals. The barn swarmed with them like bees in a hive. They were very destructive to the wheat stacked in the barn. My Grand Father told me he would give me a cent for every rat I would catch in his barn. I induced my Father to buy me two new steel traps. He paid 37½ cents apiece for them. They were first rate ones. When they snapped on a rat, they held him tight, and no mistake. They never self-surrendered their victims. That was done by the boy rat-master. I soon tried the traps, as a boy would, and in a day or two, the scalps of twenty-five rats brought me (jubilant was I) the first Spanish quarter I ever owned. My success in the business rapidly brought me : such an inflow of Spanish quarters that I no longer wondered at the wealth of Stephen Girard, or the riches of Jacob Aster: for rats were plentiful, and my income enormous. I continued the avocation for weeks, and then discontinued the occupation, still leaving a few remaining rats that seemed to have no affinity for my traps. So many of their numbers disappearing, I suppose they imagined some one of superior sagacity must be ensnaring them. Thus were the rats mostly banished from the barn, and my office made prdigiously profitable. Neither Stephen nor Jacob were as jubilant over their millions, equal to my tin box of quarters. It was a most remarkable thing for a boy, in those early days, to have a handful of white Spanish quarters. They were seen by all the boys in the Valley. It was not then customary, fashionable, or popular, to give boys, or young folks money. If they got the exquisite gingercake once, or twice a year, it was amply sufficient for their services. Even the big folks, or old folks, were seldom the proprietors, or sole owners of a few pieces of coin. Debts were mostly paid in exchanged labors; or a Swine's ham; or a quarter of beef; or a "grist"; or a few bushels of potatoes etc., etc.,

The boys of the Valley wished they were in my shoes, so that their pocket
books (if they had any) could jingle a little from the profits accuring
from the squealing and scalping of rats.

CHAPTER XV

In my boyhood days there were no churches in the Valley. The
first church was built in 1828, near Salona, at the graveyard. Having
been occupied about 30 years, it was vacated and removed, and a new one
built at Salona. Previous to 1828 all church services were held in
private houses and barns. Very early in life, my Father took me by the
hand and led me to the various services held in the M. E. Church. One
Sabbath evening at a prayer meeting held in a barn, I sat beside a young
man recently converted. During prayer, he exhorted me to seek the Lord.
I prayed and became very Happy. I believed I was soundly converted.
But revealing my feelings to no one, I did not join the church, and con-
sequently declined in my religious feelings. Indeed, in those primitive
days, it was generally thought, that religion rather belonged to the
old folks. Not much attention was given to the religion of children.
The first Sabbath School established, was an impressive, memorable epoch
in the children and youth of Nittany Valley. It was organized in 1827
at Salona by the Rev. Edward E. Allen, a young Methodist Preacher from
the City of Baltimore. It was his first year in the Baltimore Conference.
It is, perhaps, the oldest Sabbath School in any of the adjacent counties.
The school was held in an old log school house on the hill side south of
the present Salona. The exercises of the school consisted in reading the
scriptures, and committing verses to memory, for which the scholars were
rewarded by giving them a blue ticket (a scripture verse) for committing
five scripture verses, and a red ticket for committing twenty verses.
Values in cents were placed on these blue and red tickets, and when the
scholars had a sufficient number of them, they bought a New Testament or
Bible. This was a great victory! A Triumph! There was not, perhaps,

one Library book, at that day, published in the United States. I think
Rev. John P. Durbin D.D. a Methodist Preacher, published the **first**
Library book in 1821. The Rev. E. E. Allen took a great interest in
the school. Everytime he came round on the circuit, he would visit the
school and talk to us. He was greatly beloved by the scholars and
teachers. When he left the circuit, and paid us his last visit, he
gave us a farwell address, shook hands with all the scholars, and had us
promise to be good. As he took each one by the hand he would say, "Dont
forget your promise." We all wept. Rev. E. E. Allen was one of the
best men I ever knew, but he had cultivated the unpleasant habit of
"rolling up the white of his eyes" when he was praying or preaching.
Perhaps it had a good effect afterall, for I was sure he was looking
up at the angels, and saw them.

CHAPTER XVI

His colleague Rev. Amos Smith, was rather a cross, surly,
exacting. I had little fondness for him. I went some distance, one
night, in company with some young people to hear him preach. He gave
it to the sinners terribly. He said he would not be surprised if the
devil would catch sinners that were in the house, on the road, before
they got home. I was young and greatly alarmed: for I thought then,
that all a preacher said, came down from above and was true. When I
got out of the house, I caught hold of the largest fellows coat skirt,
holding on tight all the way home, and looking every way, every moment
to see if the devil was coming with rams or ox horns. But the old
gentleman didn't find us, and we made our escape home in safety. No
apology can be given by the pulpit, for such unpleasant thrusts, rude-
ness, gruffness, and falsehoods. Another Preacher (Oliver Age) once
spoke to me unbecomingly. I was working for a farmer, one summer, I
was then about eleven or twelve years old. I was ploughing on rough

ground, and had some difficulty in managing the plow. The Preacher, at the supper table, asked me "if it did not make me swear when the plow would not go right." I was very timid and made no reply. I was surprised at his remark to think I would swear. My conscience was tender, and I was a type of innocency. I have despised his remark ever since, and not held him in highest estimation. Near our house, on a hill side, a piece of new road was made, and leveled up on lower side by large stones not laid very close together. One day I was passing along the road, and heard a curious sound under the stones. I never heard such a noise before. I got a little short stick, and reaching in, I felt something moving my stick. I punched a long time in the hole, and was greatly amused to learn, that the more I severly punched, the more noise it made. At last, I went and told my Mother about it. She came and removed the stone, and found a large black rattle snake coiled lying there. She killed it. I said, I didn't know that snakes had bells on their tails. We had a fine lot of two or three acres, which was largely overgrown, one summer, with a noxious, offensive yellow weed. My Father a Mill Wright, being generally away from home, he told me on Monday morning, as he left, if I would pull up all those yellow weeds, that week, out of the lot, he would bring me a large ginger-cake on Saturday evening. Oh! The exquisite ginger-cake. I was jubilant over the contract. The reward was a stimulus and ample. For the ginger-cake was a high prize in those days. It has never been higher. Soon the first weeds were up, but "there were more to follow". Most faithfully did I tug and tear up the dregs through six, long, hot, summer days, without vacant hours for rest. The coming Saturday evening, in constant anticipation, gave muscle, zest, and enjoyment to the undertaking. The last evening brought the expected reward.

31

CHAPTER XVII

In my boyhood days, it was the custom of all the families in the Valley to raise Flax. We sowed, yearly, from a half to three quarters of an acre. The flax furnished our linens for clothing. All, young and old, were apparalled in it. The webs were strong, substantial, and permanent. The calicoes, more ornamental, were for church-going on Sunday to those who could afford them. The flax was sowed after the manner of wheat. When fully grown, it's maturity was indicated by the complexion. It was then pulled up, by hand, from the roots, and spread out, exposed to the weather for a few weeks, so that the woody fibres would decay and become brittle. It was then gathered up in small bundles, and submitted, by hand, to an instrument called a "Brake", to thrash or beat out the woody fibres in the flax. To further remove the remaining fibres, the flax was scutched, as it was called. To accomplish this, a board about a foot wide and four feet long, was placed vertically in the ground, on which a bunch of the broken flax was laid, held by the hand, and beaten with a wooden stick in the form of a case knife, called a scutch. The last process con-sisted in drawing the flax through an instrument or comb with iron teeth, to remove the tow from the flax. These various processes com-pletely removed all the fibres and tow from the flax, and made it ready for the spinning wheel. Now, the mother, after the toils of the day, spends her winter evenings at the wheel, turning her flax into threads, and filling the spools. The bright light is furnished, not by the candle, but by the big flambeau resinous pine knot, as it stands up vertically and majestically, in the back part of the chimney. The winter spinning task completed, and the hanks colored (generally .yellow) are thrust into bags, then on horseback (no buggies in those days)' and conveyed to the weavers: the Mother accompanies the cargo to give instructions to her wishes. In a few weeks the web comes home,

and there is a family jubilee, especially among the children. What
delights! They dance, prance, hop, jump, caper, romp, skip, sport, make
merry, etc., etc., and all that and more too. They are all on the web
rolling it over the floor. No wonder. A great thing has come to our
house. It comes only once in a year. It is, especially, to attire in
beauty the girls and boys. Who shall have the first apparel, Mother?
Shall it be a frock or a pair of trousers? Where are the shears? There
they are. Hurry up. Can't wait. Now for the needle and thread. Get
my thimble. No sewing machines in those days. Well, the linens are
turned into complete outfits for all the girls and boys. The girls have
hastened over to Grandpa's to exhibit and announce their robes. The
boys are out seeing how high they can jump in their new linens. They
run through the bushes; climb saplings, leap over fences; slide down on
the rough bark of trees, which only files off the roughness and polishes
trousers. Jubilee.

CHAPTER XVIII

Those were domestic days. Days of domestic manufactures.
Home made days. Tampores mutanter! Candles were made by taking a dozen
of wicks of usual length, suspended to a round stick, then on a very cold
day, dipping the wicks down into a vessel of melted tallow. Then lifting
them out, the tallow would freeze to the wicks. This dipping was continued until the candles had the required thickness. Candles, however,
were not much used. Winter lights flamed out mostly from the richly
resinous pine knot in the chimney. The "Pine Barrens", as they were called,
(or woods) abounded in rich pine knots. Many of these knots were three
and four feet long, and from three to five and six inches in diameter.
In the fall season of the year, each family in the Valley would drive a
four-horse team with a large wagon bed to these "Pine Barrens", and get
a load of these knots for their winter chimneys. The knots were split

with the axe into quarters. We had no matches then. Matches came into
use about the year 1840. To retain fire during the night, the bed of
live coals in the chimney was covered over thickly with ashes to exclude
air. In the morning the ashes were scraped off the coals, when they
would be found almost as nice as when they were covered. If, however,
from any cause the fire should go out in the night, or at any other time,
it was obtained by striking a flint with a piece of steel or pen knife,
the spark falling on tinder, or porous, inflamable wood, called spunk.
In those olden times we had to practice economy. We had but little at
anytime, and tried to give it all the <u>longevity</u> it could have. We experienced the maxium that "Man wants, but little here below,
Nor wants that little long."

During all the week days, we supped the Rye beverage. Only
on Sunday morning we feasted on the delicious "Java". We needed no
tablecloth. The children, at meals, always waited till the two old
folks had eaten:that is the parents. They were the proprietors of the
house. The children were to come after them, which they gladly did.
When we went to Church, we carried our shoes and stockings under our
arms. It would not do to put them on: that would wear them out. When
we got near the church, we clapped them on: and when we came out of the
church, we took them off. There were no shoemaker shops in the Valley.
When the snowflakes began to fly, the shoe cobbler could be seen climb-
ing over the fence, making his way to our house, with a knapsack on his
back, to give all around a shoe outfit. He would remain two or three
weeks at the house. Our shoes were all made of cow hides, or ox hides.
The calf skin leathers were for the feet of gentlemen of cloth. If our
shoes were thick, and heavy, they had the virtue of solidity, firmness,
and durability. We didn't matter dog bites, if they thrust their teeth
only at the Oxhides.

34

CHAPTER XIX

In all my earlier years, the opportunities for school-going
were exceedingly meagre. Oftentimes, for years, we had no schools:
and generally, when we had them, we might as well been at home. Nothing
was taught us. Our chief instructions consisted in the stern command,
"Look on your books". I think I was in my sixteenth year before I went
to a school, properly dominated such. Only once in all my life did I
play truancy. I was about ten years old. In all my after years, I have
never been able to summon conscience sufficient to express a grief for
it, for it was as beneficial and delightful to me, yea, more so, than
if I had been in the school cabin: for I was blest sitting in my Grand-
Father's orchard, pleasantly reclining under a fine shady apple tree,
with my hat half full of green apples, as big as chestnuts, which I
picked up off the grass under the tree. They were all deliciously
devoured but the stems. Further reference is made to schools in those
early days, in this Volume, beginning on page 73.

CHAPTER XX

Salona, the chief town of the Valley, and near the native
place of the writer, is a flourishing Village, containing about three
hundred inhabitants, situated five miles south of the city of Lock Haven;
one hundred and nine miles north west of Harrisburg; and two hundred and
fifteen miles north west of Philadelphia. It is located in Lamar Township; about three miles from the East End of Nittany Valley in Clinton
County, Pa.

The Valley is a beautiful one, running East and West, and
about thirty miles long, and from two to five miles in breadth. Sprinkled
with towns and villages. In agricultural products, it is one of the
richest in the State. It yields rich rewards to the husbandmen. The
central part of the Valley, running East and West, and parallel with the
North and South mountains, is called "Barrens". They are high, irregular

ridges, destitute of streams of water. Outcrops of limestone render
the surface uneven. The Barrens are not quite equidistant from the
mountains, but approach more nearly the North than the South side of the
Valley, and the dip is much more abrupt than on the South side. This
ridge, or central axis is conticlinal, that is, the strata dip in two
opposite directions from the crest or summit of the ridge. Beneath the
"Barrens" lie vast accumulations of rich iron ore. The Eastern ex-
tremity of the "Barrens", vanish within a mile of the Mill Hall Gap.
From the Gap to the East End of the Valley (about four miles), the floor
of the Valley is generally level, except near the base of the mountains.
Extensive underlying beds of limestone dipping North, stretch down the
entire length of the Valley without interruption. At Salona, the Strata
becomes more horizontal. Farther East the dip rapidly increases, and the
limestone is soon carried too far beneath the surface to be profitably
worked. The Mill Hall Gap seen from the Valley, has the charm of
romantic wildness. The deep gorge, margined with bald, sand rocks, re-
fusing a carpet of verdure, amassed in confusion, immensely heightens the
grandeur of the scene. In the vicinity of Salona, several caverns have
been discovered, but nothing more valuable in them than stalactites
depending from the roof of the cavern, and stalagmites ascending from the
floor. They are sparry concretions, or carbonerous icicles. Fishing
Creek, heading in Sugar Valley, breaks through a large gap in Nittany
mountain, and by various deflections, flows North East through a highly
cultivated, productive, and populous Valley; glides near Salona; and
seeks it's outlet through the Mill Hall Gap; thence into the Bald Eagle
Creek. It's rapid declivity affords motive power for numerous manufacturing establishments. It is spanned by numerous bridges, and has several
affluents.

CHAPTER XXI

In former years trout, very plentifully, abounded in Fishing Creek, and were caught in great number. Their capture requires much skill. To the late Samuel Wilson, Esq. of Salona more honor is ascribed, than to any other man in the Valley, in being the most successful angler. In a company of sporting fishermen, he always led the van. His rod crowned him victor of the finny tribes. His genious, thoroughly studied and comprehended the instincts and habits of the cunning trout. His line never played above the waters in vain. The fly upon his hook had always a wonderful charm for the trout. His sharp eye, and quick intuition never failed to put the hook in his mouth when he came to the surface. The fish was sure to leave his native element. In earlier days his table seldom furnished an entertainment without the presence of the trout. The trout will make great efforts to overcome difficulties in ascending to fresh water. They will swim against swift, powerful currents towards head waters, and leap up dams and cascades to find their way to fresh brooks that run down hill and mountain slopes. A large, beautiful stream of clear fresh water is entirely submerged in the Lamar Gap, (South Mountain). It traverses the whole Valley obliquely through a subterranean, limestone channel, and again emerges into daylight in close proximity to Salona. It is familiarly called the "Boiling Spring". It files it's way through the Village, and empties into Fishing Creek. On the opposite side of Salona from the "Boiling Spring", another beautiful, copious fountain of pure, clear, cold water quietly looms up near the residence of the late Samuel Wilson - my Grand-Father Ferree's first home. It is about twenty feet in diameter. It's depth has never been sounded. Speckled trout, of fine dimensions, can be seen playing in it's waters. Salona is partly surrounded by a range of beautiful semi-circular, sloping highlands, declining towards the Village, and mantled with stately trees. The Village was dignified by the euphonie

title, Salona, in about the year 1830. The name was given to it by
Samuel Wilson, and not by E. Wilson as stated in the history of Clinton
County. Salona, even in it's earlier days, had weekly debates, especially in winter evenings, in school houses. Many fine minds, of
high order, engaged in these debates. They sifted propositions of great
breadth; went to the bottom of subjects; and were often eloquent. The
debates furnished entertainment and profit for leisure hours, and crowds
came to attent and enjoy them. The decisions were grounded both upon
the ability of the debates, and the merits of the questions. Spurious
arguments and sophisms were often routed with great amusement, by out-
breaks of wit and sound logic. The Robinsons, William and Alexander,
were naturally talented in merriment. If they could twist even a good
argument out of it's groove for the sake of a little sport, they would
cheerfully sacrifice the logic for the fun. Alexander hailed from the
mountain, and often came to the debate partially robed in the raw skin of
some animal: his oddities in debates and costume produced great merriment among the young folks. To Salona very especially belongs the un-
doubted honor of bestowing careful attention to the intellectual and
moral culture of her youth. The fruits of this wise vigilence are seen
in the rich rewards of splendid names that adorn her citizens in the
various walks of life, and the grand array of her distinguished sons and
daughters that are honoring their respective professions. It challenges
comparison with any other village in the State. It is very remarkable,
and in a high degree praise-worthy that no licensed hotel has ever been
tolerated in Salona. All praise is due to the citizens, whose moral
tone has always excluded these legal, pernicious nuisanses from the
midst of them. It is perhaps, unparalleled in any other town in the
State. Hence Salona has never been eminent in bacchanalian minstrelsies.
The midnight voices of convivial fellows, merry with wine, have never
echoed from her halls. Grog-songs, the fruits of chimng glasses and

whiskey bottles, have never disturbed the nightly quiet of the streets.

CHAPTER XXII

No jovial concerts of those who "tarry long at the wine"; babble out their drinking, saloon lyrics in the town of Salona. The courts make no legal drafts; issue no legal writs or warrants on drunkards for crimes committed there in fits of intoxication. No criminal in jail or penitentiary points to saloons in Salona, where he first began to imbibe the intoxicating lebations. The eyes of the children and youth of Salona gaze not in wonder upon the bloated, staggering attitudes of the drunkard, whose pitiable plight is the legitimate fruit of the Law granting the bewitching poison.

CHAPTER XXIII

These sketches would be incomplete without some references to schools in my early days. Prior to the establishment of the public schools in Pennsylvania, in 1834, schools were sustained by personal subscriptions: the patron paying from one to two dollars per quarter for each pupil subscribed. There was no regular time for school to commence. Each school was totally separate from all the others. There was no unity, no associations of schools, no Institutes, and no supervision of any kind over them. Neither teachers, nor books, or methods or qualifications, in anything were required, as to fitness. There was no preference of school grounds for a school house. There was no choice selected for it's location. Any place, however unattractive and rough, among rocks and stumps, and hillsides, and blacksmiths' lofts was good enough for a school house. It was sometimes located on wagon roads, or in a lane or alley, or commons, or far out in an open field, away from shrubs and flowers, and shade trees, and from everything else that is beautiful and lovely, and that would attract the little feet that gathered there. Only the shadows of the old dead oak were thrown upon the little domicile:and it's leafless boughs were

the favorite resort of the owl, hawk, and buzzard. No white fence en-
closed the grounds, nor beautiful walks, nor verdure, nor one of a thousand
things that could have adorned these rude temples of learning. In summer
the little cabin itself furnished shadows for the numerous swine that
nestled around it: and when unoccupied, it was the accustomed resort or
habitation of sheep within. When I was quite a small boy, under my "teens"
our house was near one of these literary domiciles, or little log colleges.
It was fine sport for the little fellow, sometimes, to quietly hasten to
the little domicile, filled with sheep, and suddenly spring into the sheep
fold, without giving any previous notice to the quietly reposing inmates
and vigorously flutter a bush well filled with dry leaves, and a loud,
respectable shout, quickly brought the assembly to their feet. In the
general bustle there was no delay in their getting quickly out into the
fresh air. The boy was delighted to imagine that each one in his rapid exit,
was entitled to a gentle rap as he leaped over the high, rickety benches.
The same boy, on one of these occasions, sprang a sudden alarm upon the
fleecy tribe, which brought them quickly to their feet, for their outward
movement. The pioneers of the flock safely made their outward escape
through the door. But, in the hurry, a number, at once crowded in the door
way, and became so tightly wedged in that they had quite a pause, or stop in
their outward movement. One large wether, tilted on high legs, was still
within, prancing round, and casting his eyes about, philosophizing as to the
best way to make his escape. Perceiving the dilemma he was in, and imagin-
ing that there was not much time for deliberation and delay in the matter,
he concluded not to wait for the clearing away of the jam at the door,
ut to the great amazement of the boy, he made a desperate, outward leap
over all the backs of the others in the jam, sailing clear without touch-
ing bottom, but not, however, without receiving a respectable whack from
the boys stick, on the last end going out to hurry him onward.

40

So far as the writer knows, no efforts were made in the neighborhoods to
exclude the fleecy quadrupeds, and others with snouts, from their
customery resorts in these literary cabins. The "Masters" (not teachers)
as we shall call them, were generally old bachelors - traveling
cosmopolites of Irish nationality. They were usually good disciples of
the distilleries that could be seen smoking over the Valley, in those
early days, more numerous than school houses. These "fellows" or "Masters"
in their perigrinations over the country, would pause for a quarter, in
some neighborhood, and for the want of something to do, would "take up a
school" in the little "sheep cabin". Instead of "boarding round", he would
sometimes lodge in a bunk in a corner of the school house, with his
"bottle for a pillow, and buy his provisions at a farm house. If the
night did not furnish him hours enough for "nature's sweet restorer", he
would snatch a little time during the day for a "short nap" on a bench,
while the scholars were "busy getting their lessons." Taking some
"bitters" to quiet his nerves, he is quietly extended on a bench, reposing in his slumbers. When the snoring began, it was his signal that he
had already arrived at "nod-land". Now, a mischievous wight, instead of
"getting his lessons", watches his opportunity, and carefully pours some
powder on the bench about his head, and on his hair, and being an expert
with the flint, he cautiously drops a spark on the preparation. The snapp-
ing of the powder grains, with a little smoke, and a small blaze, trying
his fleece, never failed to arouse him from his slumbers. He sprang for
his "gad" to chastise the criminal who started the explosion, but he could
not be found. Nobody did it: for the scholars were all "busy getting their
lessons". Their "habitual drowsiness" was doubtless the result of the too
frequent use of the "Spirits". The "Masters" had but little, if any
qualifications for their transient vocation. It was not their profession.
They engaged in it simply for the want of something to do. Parents
committed their children to them for instruction with but little concern

for their improvement. It seemed enough for them to know that "the
School Master was abroad". And yet every facility and qualification,
including the "master" himself, for the intellectual cultivation of their
youth were wanting. For this parental neglect, perhaps we may find an
apology for them, in their being the primitive settlers of the soil: or,
at least, in time-distance not very far removed from them. Their physical
wants first claimed attention. The wilderness had first to yield to the
axe, and the soil to the plow. Various hindrances for many long years were
endured, before the rude forest life emerged into the higher and more re-
fined life. Hence, schools of any worth were of slow growth and very im-
perfect. Perhaps it would not be merely an idle curiosity, but somewhat
interesting and desirable, to make some more minute references to those
"sheep cabins", called school houses, and schools (miserable things) in
the days of our forefathers, before their history is veiled in oblivion.
Almost uniformly over the state, in those early days, especially in the
rural districts, the school houses were low, round-log cabins, one story
varying in dimensions, generally about fifteen feet by twenty feet. The
floor was made of puncheons: that is split logs with the flat sides upper-
most, and in the rough. Snakes would, sometimes, come up through the
crevices, or seams between the logs. A few scattered, loose slabs over-
head, on cross logs, formed the ceiling, or inner flooring above. The roof
was covered with heavy, rough clapboards, split from ack logs, and kept
down upon the roof by laying heavy poles or logs on them. Heavy rains
would often filter down through the vents or crevices of the clapboards,
and produce a busy commotion of the urchins beneath. The seams between
the unbarked, round logs in the walls were filled with blocks and chips
and sticks, tightly driven in, and smeared over with mud to exclude the
cold, and air, and snowflakes. At one end of the cabin, one half the
length of the end logs was left out, for the use of the chimney. The
chimney was made of wooden sticks, placed crosswise upon one another, and

daubed inside and out with mortar. The chimney was often more than half
the breadth of the house. It was sometimes so large, that heavy logs of
wood were dragged into the chimney of the school house by a horse.
For tongs, a huge poker of the hand-spike kind, was a substitute. If no
chimney beautified the domicile, an old iron ten-plate stove was substituted, with a piece of stove pipe just long enough to extend through
the ceiling into the loft above. The caged smoke greatly taxed it's
ingenuity to get out through the crevices of the clapboards. What refused to escape in that way angrily returned, impartially visiting the
eyes of the urchins below. But, as that was a utilitarian age, even the
smoke was utilized. For oftentimes a farmers' wagon would pause at the
door of the schoolhouse, in school hours, well loaded with hams and
chunks of beef, and lots of sausages on their way to iron hooks and nails
on the school house loft, and there remain suspended until sufficiently
smoked. On two sides of the house, opposite each other, were the windows.
For this purpose, a log or two was taken out of each side of the house,
making the windows about ten feet long and a foot wide. Across the open
space, small sticks of wood were placed for windows. Frequently in the
absence of panes of glass for the windows, thin white paper panes were
substituted. The paper was greased to make it more translucent. If one
of the paper panes became broken, or during the night it's greasy quality
was tested by the mice, another piece of paper out of Jim's copy book was
substituted, and greased with a little butter out of Peter's dinner
basket. The door was made after the fashion of a barn door, with wooden
hinges, a wooden latch, and a leather string on the outside to lift it.
Black boards had not yet been invented. And even if they had been, they
would of been of no use in those days. Even in many after years, in
many places , objections were made to their introduction. There were no
desks for scholars in those days. The benches on which they sat were all
made of slabs from the saw-mill, unplaned, the flat sides turned up.

43

Holes were bored through the ends, and large round sticks of wood were
driven in them for legs. The benches were all of the same height for
scholars little and big. They had no backs. They were the length of the
house and placed parallel: that is equally distant apart, and no isles
at all between them. The scholars had to blimb over them. On these
high, long slabs, without backs, children would sit all the day long,
generally with their faces buried in their books, to conceal the fearful frowns of the "Master". No recesses were ever given. There reclined
the weary little ones, with aching limbs, and dangling feet, hoplessly
aiming to touch the floor, until the tiresome hours of the closing day
brought them their coveted, sweet relief. Their only remedy and hope, in
time to come, was in the coming years that would furnish them longer legs.
For writing desks, holes were bored in the side logs of the house, under
the windows, and strong wooden plugs were driven in them. On these
plug sticks, a slab was laid, the flat side up, unplaned. This was the
pupil's writing desk. There were no copy-books in those days, no printed
copies to imitate. Their copy-books consisted of a few sheets of coarse
foolscap. The "Master" set all the copies. No ruled lines were on the
paper. The lines were ruled by the "Master", or scholars with raw lead,
wedge-shaped, hammered out from a bullet. Neither were there any steel
pens in those days. The "Master" made pens for all the scholars out of
goose quills furnished by the scholars: gander's quills did just as well.
Before school, in the morning, the geese in the neighborhood bould be seen
on the wing, flying in all directions, being hotly pursued by the young
tyros for their quills. In winter, bundles of quills could be seen suspended in chimney corners "drying", awaiting the sharp pen knife of the
"Master". The "bundles" were trophies, memorials of conquests, evincing
the young "Perts" victors, in their contests with the "Ganders".

The inks were all home-made. Utilitarian boys would make red
ink out of poke-weed juice. No matches in those days. They were invented

in about the year 1840. In the winter morning, the "Master" would walk
a mile, more or less, through the deep snows, carrying hot coals on his
shovel to make his school house fires. I have doen this hundreds of
times, plowing through snows two and three feet deep, over fields, climb-
ing fences, through snow storms, and without any broken snow path. I
may as well also say, that my pen knife has sharpened the ends of many
scores of bundles of goose and gander quills, and scores of other achievements alluded to in these sketches. For the reader may as well know that
I commenced my "Vital spark" sometime back. I have been running in the
Flint-Mill about four score years, and seen things new and old. In my
earlier school days, the whole range of studies embraced spelling, reading, writing and arithmetic. No other branches of study were taught or
known in the Valley. A leaf, with the alphabet upon it, was pasted on a
shingle, and kept close to the "Master". The pupil was called up to the
"Master", and repeated it after him several times a day, until he had
committed it to memory, if it took all the winter to complete the task.

        Neither amusing nor improving exercises were associated with
it. When his eye was off the shingle, he was idle, entirely unoccupied,
and ready for mischief when the "Master's" eye was not upon him. Pupils
were kept in the spelling book until they had thoroughly mastered it.
Spelling was a specialty. Evening Spelling Schools in the school houses
were frequent, and occasions of great amusement and profit. Choosing sides,
and "spelling down" were the accustomed methods. The English Grammar of
the celebrated Lindley Murray, although a Pennsylvanian, born in Lancaster
County, was but little known in his own State for many years after it's
publication. Also the very popular English Grammar of Samuel Kirkham was
but little known in even Central Pennsylvania for years, although Kirkham taught school in Lewisburg, Danville, and Northumberland, and wrote
his Grammar while teaching in those places.

45

There was no choice of books, in those days, for schools. The almost
entire encyclopedia of school books was embraced in Dilworth's and
Byerly's spelling books; Lindley Murray's introduction to his English
Reader; his sequal; and Daboll's, Dilworth's and Pike's Arithmetics.
There was no classification of studies, especially in writing and arithmetic. Scholars generally recited to the "Master" separately. There was
often as many classes as Scholars.

Recesses for scholars, those transient happy recreations in
the middle of half days, had not yet been discovered. Scholars were ex-
cused to be absent from the schoolroom one at a time. The scholar indicated his wish by screaming aloud, "May I go out?" When one hand of
the pupil was on the door latch, the other hand, by the law of the
"Master", was required to grasp a shingle from a nail in the log, and turn
the other side facing the school. On it was printed in large letters, the
word "Out". When he returned to the school room, he again turned the
shingle, that all eyes could see the word, "In" written upon it. This
was a laconic device, and indicated in a simple way the presence of all,
or the absence of one.

In Arithmetic, when scholars reached "the single rule of
three", they were accounted "Proficients". If they attained the "double
rule three" they were profound Arithmeticians. No rules were learned,
nor were any explanations ever given by the "Master". If the scholar
caould not "work the sum", the "Master" would solve it, if he could, and
return the slate to the scholar without any explanation. No reasons were
given for the solutions. Facts only were to be known, but not the reason
of the facts. Perhaps, in most cases, the "Master", himself, knew as little
about the reasons as the scholar. It would have been a gross insult,
and cost the scholar a severe "flogging", if he dared to be so familiar
and impudent as to ask the "Master" why it was so.

In those early times schools were generally kept during the holidays of "Christmas" and "New Year". Barring the "Master" out of the school house on those merry-making days, was a favorite sport among the scholars. To accomplish this amusement, the scholars, early in the morning, would hasten to the school house before the "Master" arrived, all get within doors, and strongly "bar" the door and windows to keep the "Master" out when he came. When he arrived, they refused his admission until he promised to supply them plentifully with apples and cider. This he would generally promise, and hasten away, at once, to some Farm house for the desired commodities, and quickly return with a wallet of the delicious fruit on his back, and a jug of respectable dimensions containing the exquisite beverage. After enjoying, for a time, the pleasant repast, the "Master" dismissed them for the day. Apples and cider were the only festive articles, in those days, unless we add the superior, lightly-prized "Ginger Cake."

Daniel O'Bryen, an Irish school "Master" of the "olden time", was very ingenious in devising schemes of relief in such "barring out" emergencies. He would climb up on the roof of the school house, and throw sulphur down the chimney, on the fire, and cover the top of the chimney with boards. Daniel, on the top of the chimney, fondly imagined there was sufficient virtue in the fumes of his sulphur to speedily fling open the door below. This Daniel's prohibited ingress was skilfully made possible. The "Master" was the great presiding genius of the school room. He was verily "monarch of all he surveyed". Most frequently his face, that children so quickly read and decern was richly adorned with a fine crop of grog-blossoms. Nothing would so soon startle the youth of a neighborhood, as the sudden arrival of one of these traveling pedagogues, "going round" with a subscription paper for a school. The natural impulses of the youth revolted against the prospective tyranny that was sure to follow. By common consent, he was invested with plenipotentiary

power. He was a tall figure; Roman nose (sword-like); clad in leather
buck-skins, the lower extremities of which were urged down into a pair
of high, oxhide boots. His cap which he always kept on his head in the
school, was made of a red fox skin, the hair of which was without, and the
bushy tail furnished the ornamental cue behind. The other outfits were
in harmony with them. He presided over the terror-stricken innocents
within, with a dominant authority that would not have justified a military Ruler of Australian criminals. Under his left arm was always tightly
clenched a rod of fine dimensions. It never left him. It was his
principal badge of office. The condition that he had muscle to "play it
well", was the chief qualification of his vocation. It was the best and
most important piece of apparatus in the school room, and the busiest.
With this valuable instrument in his long arm, he could experiment upon
a boy in the most distant part of the school room without leaving his
split-bottomed arm chair. So true was his aim in the business, from
experience, that he could raise the dust from a boys' jacket at every
stroke of his long "gad". Often, for the offence of one, he would
soundly "birch" the whole school. Good lessons were generally fruits
of his frowns, rather than for love or fondness of the book. He was more
careful in inventing modes of punishment than in devising means for
instruction. When he was unusually disturbed, especially for the want
of his "bitters", his temper would ruffle at the slightest incident.
Look out! Hold your breath! He's coming. He is liable to explode at
any time. It was, then, his general habit to quickly pace up and down
the little aisle, pelting occasionally some little foot with the toe of
his boot. The scholars, accustomed to similar spasms, prophesied the
coming storm. The "Master" unable longer to endure the pent up steam,
snatches his "ox gad" as the boys "christened" it, and circuits the whole
school room, giving each boy and girl a respectable "whack". There was
unusual silence on those occasions. No sound was heard, but the music

of the "gad" as it whistled through the air. Each one, boys and girls,
awaited, but not coveted his or her turn. The smoke on jackets, from
strokes, sometimes, plentifully floated in the sunbeams shining through
the windows. Various were his modes of punishment. The little offender,
for amusing himself with a fly, was called to the front, and go down
on all "fours", elephant - like. The"Master"now laid a billet of wood
on his back, which, for a long time was to be delicately balanced and
endured, until the young philosopher, in that way, had sufficiently
atoned for his crime. "Bill", for putting up his fore finger to bump
"Tom's" nose as he turned round, was made to stand out on the floor
on one foot, facing the "Master", and the other foot projected straight
out in the opposite direction, to balance a block of wood held out at
armslength in one hand. Sometimes a large boy would carry another on
his back around the stove for his offence. The writer, very well re-
members , that when he was a small boy, and had offended his "magister-
ial Royalty", was made to climb up on the late Rev. Daniel Hartman's
back, and describe Elliptic curves around the stove. The punishment was
ample for trying to catch a fly. If the offence was a grievous one,
he was carried around the house on the outside. This method of traveling without, was no little amusing to the young culprit, who was very
vigilent in concealing his smiles from the "Master" within. Perhaps,
in his revolutions around the house outside, he was as profitably employed as if he had been within.

Sometimes a goose quill was split, and put on a boy's nose,
while standing out on the floor on one foot, with his hands behind his
back. Sometimes a strap, long and wide, cut from a bear's skin, with
the long, black wool still on one side, with eye holes punched through
it, was a favorite article with the "Master". He carried it in his
pocket. When a lad was arraigned before him, and the "Master's" hand
went into his pocket, all the scholars, from experience, had been

educated to know, that he had gone there after his "Spex": silence
reigned. The boy's lips quivered; the tears came, but obsequious
(the strap never returned void) faithful in it's mission, it was sure to
make it's way to the boy's nose and eyes. A good lesson could be dis-
pensed with, by the "Master", for enjoying the luxury of clapping a
fleecy strap from the raw hide of old "bruin" on a boy's nose. It gave
the boy a frightful appearance. Many of the young children would cry
at the spectacle. Some had the superstitious idea, that there was a
bear behind the "Spex". Sometimes a boy on his knees, was required to
creep over the floor, under the benches, and push an empty bucket with
his head.

It was common to strike heavy blows, with a ruler, on the
palm of one or both hands. Oftentimes the ends of the thumb and fingers
were placed tightly together, and so forcibly struck with a heavy ruler,
that the nails seemed driven in to the flesh.

Such were a few of the many modes of school punishment,
practiced by most of the "Master's of the olden times". It is somewhat remarkable that even in that early day, parents would allow their
children to receive such brutal treatment without complaint, and utter-
ing their revengeful protests. But, it must not be thought that all
the "Masters" of those early times were of this baser sort. Many were
true and noble, model teachers (primary though they were) as were
prevalent in their day. In these descriptions therefore, our vocation
is not all fault-finding. Many things we state as facts, which were
disreputable. It is charitable to suppose that many did what they
could faithfully. In most cases they imperfectly laid rude foundations:
nevertheless we have built upon them. We now rear magnificant school
temples of learning, adorned and beautified by all that science can
reveal, and art can furnish.

In our part of the Valley, the last link of these floating Cosmopolites, these leisurely traveling pedagogues, was followed by the inauguration of Samuel Wilson (of Salona) as an instructor. He was unusually active, and fleet as a deer on foot. In a race-game with the scholars, boys and young men, he would skim over the surface like a swift-winged bird, When in swift pursuit to overtake a rival, he seemed to young eyes, to be on the wing coming and sweeping by with the velocity of an arrow. Light first began to dawn in the school room, when he became our presiding genius. He was the best reader in the Valley. Under his instructions the old forms and methods in the school room began to retire, and were banished. A reformation in school work set in; progress in the right direction was written on our banners, and a higher order of things established. We are happy to know, that the little log colleges and rude "Masters", and books have all vanished away. They but imperfectly served our Fore Fathers. We live comparatively in a golden age. A better era has dawned upon us. Twilight has vanished. The sun has risen in his splendor. Mind is now marching rapidly. Inventions and discoveries are speedily bearing the world onward. The Temples of learning are thrown open, and all her devotees are promised reward, richer than gold, and of more value than the "revenues of choice silver". Women never taught. The public school system was not yet introduced. Reference to it will be made in a future chapter.

CHAPTER XXIV

In the summer of 1828 (in my 14th year) I was employed with my Father, in the Valley, at Mill Wright, and various other kinds of work. The first work at which we set in was repairing the McGhee Flouring Mill. It wanted a large, new shaft of great strength, as it was the chief instrumental wheel in driving and turning the other wheels of the Mill. Hence, we repaired to the woods to get out the required shaft.

51

We wanted a tree about thirty feet long, and two and a half feet in
diameter, without a limb, and carrying the same diameter through it's
entire length. We found the necessary tree and felled it. The large
cross-cut saw separated the end, and severed the shaft from the trunk.
This was tedious and hard work. This done, I was soon standing on the
mammoth log with axe in hand, for it must be nicely dressed. Large,
short slabs were to be split off all around. It was not to be cylind-
rical, but hexagonal, the whole length. Each side was to be six inches
wide, and smoothly planed. This being accomplished, I was again upon
the shaft with a $2\frac{1}{2}$" augur, for holes had to be bored entirely through
the shaft, and neatly and smoothly chiseled out about one foot long and
three inches wide. Three of these perforations were to be made quite
through the shaft, intersecting each other. Through these openings,
arms of dry, hard oak plank were made to fit, with such neatness, beauty,
and accuracy, and strength, that it seemed they had grown in that way.
On the extremities of these arms, the segments containing the cogs were
most firmly secured. The oak planks themselves, were often in a great
twist, and had to be planed "out of wind", as my Father called it: and
being of hard, dry oak, the task was by no means an easy one for a small
boy. I have been somewhat minute in this description, to indicate the
heavy work of this one piece of Mill-Wright mechanism. Repairing saw
mills was also a part of our summer's labor. The fall of this year,
1828, James Harris of Bellefonte, Center Co., Pa., contracted with my
Father to repair his Flouring Mill, and then run it the remainder of
the year. Mr. Harris was a gentleman of wealth, education, and culture,
and sho was the chief Civil Engineer in the construction and superin-
tendance of the Pennsylvania Canal. My Father therefore moved to
Bellefonte in the spring of 1829, to enter upon his contract. The
repairs being completed, my Father ran the Mill. I was now in my
fifteenth year. I aided my Father very considerably this year in

grinding out grain, and especially wheat, and in packing Superfine
Flour in barrels for the City market, and, indeed in general Mill Work.
In the winter when the mill was running constantly, and very heavily,
with three or four burrs or hoppers in motion, I attended the mill one
half of the night, and my Father the other half. I have often wondered
how a boy of my years could accomplish what I did. While I carefully
superintended all the wheat hoppers that were running vigorously in the
night, I was at every leisure moment busily packing barrels of Superfine Flour; weighing them; branding them; and heading them up ready for
the City markets. I was also an expert in hoisting up bags of three
bushels of wheat off wagons up three and four stories in the mill, then
conveying the bags away to distant granaries for deposition. I could
pick the burrs: that is, with fine steel hammers, dress and sharpen the
furrows for better grinding. Here, I met with an accident or incident
which came very near proving fatal. My younger brother, Joel, and myself, got into a small, leaky, rickety boat to fish in the mill dam.
A deep, wide, rapid currant ran near the shore. In crossing the currant,
the boat sunk and turned bottom upwards. My brother being nearer the
boat, climbed up on the bottom of the boat, and thus floated down to
the breast of the dam and got off the boat. I, being on the inside
edge of the currant, from the shore, caught a weed whose top came to
the surface of the water. The water buoyed me up vertically, coming
just to my shin. I stood in the deep water in that position, until my
brother floated down to the breast of the dam, and crawled off the
bottom of the boat, and ran in the Mill to tell Father about me. He
hastily ran for the boat, and came to my rescue. I have always deemed
my deliverance Providential.

53

CHAPTER XXV

My Father having completed his year at the Bellefonte Flouring Mill, returned again to the Valley. Part of this summer, 1830, I
worked with my Father, and for several months I worked on a farm. The
Farmer was very rigorous, covetous, domineering and exacting. He
found it difficult to get work enough out of even an industrious and
faithful boy. In the morning while it was yet quite early and dark,
he would knuckle tremendously on the head-board of his bedstead where
he slept, and yell at me "to be out". I slept in a room above him.
He would order me to make the fire, then go out to the pasture field
and bring in the horses and feed them. It was generally dark at these
times, and the fog so dense that I could scarcely see three yards before
me. The clover was "knee deep", and as wet with dew as if dipped in the
creek, and I also. Many times I could not find the horses, because I
could not see them on account of the fog. I would then travel about in
the wet clover, and listen to hear the clanking of the chains of their
feet, and thus determine their "whereabouts". After dinner on Saturday
he had an aptitude for Town, and a proclivity for sitting on store
boxes. Before leaving, however, he was sure to give his plowboy Saturday afternoon instruction. "Plow till five o'clock, then unhitch,
feed the horses and take them out to pasture. Then chase the hogs out
of the hill field, and stop up all the hog holes. Clean out the horse
and cow stables: cut wood for Sunday, and dig a bucket full of potatoes."
This specimen actually occurred, for the "small boy". The fall of this
year (1830) my Father built two horse power thrashing machines for
separating the grain from the straw. One machine was for Robert McCormick
below Lock Haven, at "the point", as it was called, near the junction of
the Bald Eagle Creek and the West Branch of the Susquehanna River. I
gladly, yea, jubilantly left the plow of the Farmer, and all his other
surroundings and aided my Father in building these two machines.

The other Farmer for whom we built a machine, was John Fleming who also lived below Look Haven, near the breast of the dam. No such machines had ever been in our part of the country. They are now quite common in Farmer's barns. Previous to the intorduction of these machines, wheat was thrashed out by horses tramping it. The sheaves were laid round the outside of the barn floor, and spans of horses traveled round on it until all the grain was tramped off out of the heads of the wheat. The horses were then removed, and the straw was shaken with a fork to filter out the wheat from it: it was then thrown out into the barn-yard. Then another layer was put down, as at first, and similarly tramped by the horses, etc., until the thrashing of the Farmer's crop was completed. The chaff was then winnowed away from the wheat by the Farmer's Wind Mill.

My Grandfather Haslet having died this summer, 1830, I arranger with my Aunt Jane Haslet, who still lived in the old home-stead, (of whom I have formerly made reference) to board with her dur-ing the winter and go to school from there. As a compensation for boarding, I was to cut the wood; make the fires; and do many other chores of light household work. Our school was in the further East End of Nittany Valley about two miles from my boarding place. Our school was the best in the Valley: indeed, the best we ever had. Our Teacher was Mr. Harvey French from New York State. I studied all the branches he taught there. I took up Pike's Arithmetic and finished it. All it's examples, and problems were in English Sterling money. There were no exerciese in dollars and cents. This was very objectionable, as our currency was in dollars and cents. The first Arithmetic we had in Federal money, was published by Isaac Torbert, a Teacher in Belle-fonte. It was a very practical and valuable little work. Under Mr. French, I took up Samuel Kirkham's English Grammar. This, to my very great regret, I did not quite complete before the session of school

ended. Mr. French took a very great interest in me. He told me that
if I would remain after school in the evening, he would give me another
extra lesson in English Grammar. This I gladly agreed to. Then again
he told me, that if I would come down to his boarding house in the
evening after supper, he would give me another lesson in the Grammar.
This I again gladly accepted. So I speedily hurried home to my boarding place, did all my evening chores, ate my supper, and away I fled
two miles with Grammar in hand for my third lesson in English Grammar.
This was daily. One evening after school, Mr. French said to me, after
the Grammar lesson "you ought to prepare yourself for a Teacher." This
remark was most unexpected, and shocked me. It was a blow from which
I recovered with difficulty. The teaching vocation I considered so
supreme, that I thought I could never attain it. The advice at the
time startled me: but it has since somewhat worn or vanished away.
Afterwards I really did enter upoon the Profession, and the instructions of fifty-five years in it, (from 1833 to 1888) have partially
dissipated the shock. In the spring of 1831, my Father left the Valley
finally, and removed to Mill Hall where he permanently resided the
remainder of his life, with transient exeptions. This summer I again
assisted him in his mechanical work. He and Robert Dougherty, another
Mill-Wright, and nephew by marriage of my Father, contracted with
George Bressler to build his Furnace in Mill Hall. In the coming winter
I attended school a few weeks on the River hill, called "Boyd's Hill"
sometimes. It was kept by Mr. Bartram, and did not amount to much.
Another school started in for a brief time, which I attended, near the
residence of Uncle George Bressler in spring of 1832. It was kept by
a Mr. Patterson. He was cross, crusty, and crabbed. He had inherited
quite a share of the asperities and crispness of the old "Masters".
The "gad" was in almost constant use. It got but little rest: never
got rusty. It's music was heard all the day long. His school was not

a sucess, although his education was quite respectable. This spring
Dr. Ely Parry and his wife, relatives of Uncle Bressler and Father,
and many others in the Valley, came up from Lancaster City. He was a
Physician and Dentist: a very superior one. He brought a box of
dentist tools with him, and did considerable work in that line while
he was up here. He plugged two front teeth for me in gold; that was
sixty years ago, and the gold plugs are in firmly yet. I said, Doctor
what is the charge? He said, "Well Wesley, if I charge you anything,
I suppose I ought to charge you two dollars". I gladly paid him his
price. This was the last summer I was with my Father among the edge-
tools, assisting him in his work of machinations. Our employment this
summber, was in making machines for cutting straw very short for horse
feed. It was a grand invention, a fine device, "something new under
the sun". The Patent was purchased by Mr. Armstrong Smith, whose
occupation was a harness and saddle maker. We made a great many
machines for him that summer. The machine was a self-feeder with straw.
The sharp, cutting knives were very firmly secured to two opposite
arms of a cast iron wheel about three feet in diameter. The wheel was
turned by hand after the manner of a grindstone. It rapidly and neatly
shaved or cut off the straw about an inch long.

Mr. Smith had two workmen in his harness shop: one a journeyman, Henry Crooks, and the other, David Clark, an apprentice. They
made me a very neat, little trunk, and put the initials of my name
upon it, in little, brass nails: thus "J.W.F." That is sixty years
ago; they are still firmly on it, and I have carried the key most of
the time in my pocket, and have it yet. The little trunk is still in
use, and in good condition.

Mr. Smith was a strict Presbyterian. The Methodist Church
was but a few rods from his residence. The sounds of the Methodists
were a little too loud for him. When they became a little noisy, as

they sometimes did, Mr. Smith would grunt our a repulsive, unsavory negative, saying, "There the Methodists are raising the black cat again".

One evening my Uncle Joel's two apprentices, John and Adam were at our house. My Mother was going to make soap and wanted more ashes. So she told us to take a bag and the boat, and go down the creek and get some from a neighbor. Adam always claiming a little of Samson's strength, shouldered the bag and staggered off with it. He put one foot in the boat, pushing it out. His feet being too far apart, he fell backwards into the water about three feet deep: the bag across his breast. He kicked and struggled mightily but the bag wouldN't budge. When we thought he was sufficiently soaked, we took the bag off him. He loomed up to the surface, the liquid pouring off him in streams. The incident furnished an amusing theme for reference many times afterward for the boys.

CHAPTER XXVI

As it was not my intention to make my Father's occupation my vocation for life, I began to determine what should engage my attention. I was disinclined to select a Profession that would require a shop, and many expensive tools of workmanship. My Uncle Joel Ferree, my Father's brother, being a Plasterer, having learned his trade in Lancaster City, and a very superior mechanic, advised me to learn the Plastering trade, saying, he often made five dollars a day. This seemed to me to be enormous wages, and impressed me most favorably in that direction: so much so, that I actually selected it as my life Profession. My Uncle, however, not just wanting an apprentice at the time, (having two) I applied to George Moore who had married my Father's cousin, Miss Charlotte Herr. He lived in Williamsburg, Huntingdon Co., Pa., about sixty miles away. He wrote to me that "he would take me,

and wished me to come at once". I soon packed my little trunk, bid
the members of the Family "good bye", leaving my Mother weeping. She
always wept when I left, and shouted when I came home. It was now
September, 1832, and I was soon in the stage, and on my journey to my
destination. The first day I reached Bellefonte, twenty miles from
home. The second day, and somewhat in the night, I arrived within
four miles of my goal: having traveled, the second day, nearly forty
miles by stage. I lodged for the night at a Hotel kept my Mr. Kin-
Kaid. It was on a beautiful turnpike road leading from Philadelphia
to Pittsburg. In the morning I left for Williamsburg, my new home.
The Family hailed me with delight. I had known them before, as they
had formerly lived in our Valley. Here I found an apprentice who
completed his plastering trade that fall. His name was Christian
Hanawalt. They were just completing the plastering of a new, brick
Methodist Church when I arrived. We did not accomplish a great amount
of work that fall. I found that my "new Master" was naturally inclined
to take the "world easy". He had a proclivity for the shops, and
frequent inclinations to pause along the streets and rest on store
boxes, and spin yarns. Warm days especially had a relaxing effect upon
his system, the shadows which the kind awnings threw down upon the pave-
ments, were pleasant and genial. They held him attractively in the
afternoons, till the ringing of the supper bell called him reluctantly
away. The winter setting in, I returned home to go to school. John
Thompson, a local Methodist Preacher taught in Salona that winter. I
went to him. He was a good man, and an excellent Teacher and Preacher.
In a few years afterwards, pulmonary troubles took away his life. He
died in great peace.

The spring having arrived, (1833) the school closed, and I
hastened to make preparations for my departure back again to Williamsburg. I was now accompanied by my Father's cousin, Uriah Herr, who was

also going with me as an apprentice to learn the Plastering trade.
Our work during the summer was meagre and contracted. There was plenty
of work to do, and we, as apprentices, were anxious to be learning,
and it would also have been profitable for the Family, yet we were
idle much of the time, because our "Master", as stated above, was in-
disposed to push business, and yet, financially poor. Uriah and I
had made some sacrifice to go out there; our trip wearisome; our time
valuable; the days passing away without profit, we were no little
discouraged. To economize as much as possible, we decided, and did
actually take our trip of sixty miles on foot, with heavy knapsacks on
our backs. Frequently, with a blush of shame, we would step to the
roadside to let the rapidly flying stage pass by with it's comfortable
smiling passengers within, while we, poor Pedestrians, were wearily
plodding our way on foot through mud, not daring to anticipate the hour
of sunset that would give us rest and sweet repose. This drudgery was
because we were not only a "little short", but almost wholly "short" of
the "Spondulix" or coin. The first day we reached Bellefonte a little
tired, twenty miles. The second day, we arrived at Birmingham, thirty
miles, greatly wearied, and with such stiffness in our limbs, that it
was with much difficulty we succeeded in getting upstairs to retire
for the night. We amusingly had to climb up on "all fours". The next
day we completed our destination, having met an "old darkey" on the way
playing a fiddle, and throwing in a Vocal Chorus,
                    "If you want to keep your credit up,
                     Pay the money down."

        We, this year, 1833, had the pleasure of hearing the World-
Wide Orator, the Rev. Henry B. Bascom D.D., of the Methodist Church.
He was then a Professor in the Transylvania University, in Kentucky.
He was traveling East, and paused a short time in Huntingdon and Center
Counties among his friends. His reputation as an Orator was great.
Bishop Waugh, who himself stood at the head of Orators, said of Bascom,

that, "he was the greatest pulpit Orator on the American Continent".
And that great Statesman and Orator, Henry Clay, had said that "Bascom
was the greatest Orator of the Age." These were great statements by
great men. Bascom preached on Sunday morning in the Methodist Church,
in Williamsburg. All the churches in town were emptied of their con-
gregations and preachers. They came to hear Bascom. He preached on
the Resurrection of Christ. His Text was, "Go tell my disciples that
He is risen from the dead". His division of the text was, First, the
fact, secondly, the necessity of His rising. It was the greatest
sermon I ever heard, judging from a boy's stand-point. He also
preached in Hollidaysburg, Huntingdon, Lewistown, and Bellefonte. This
year we were visited in Williamsburg by the Rev. Samuel Wakfield of
the Pittsburg Conference. He had published several, vocal musical
works. He was not preaching then. The following winter he taught a
number of musical schools in our country. His books were largely used.
He has since published a work on Theology. He still lives - 94 years
old. A camp meeting was held this fall near a little town called
Warrior's Mark. Uriah and I attended it. On Sabbath a Roman Catholic
Priest, who lived in Huntingdon, went up to a Catholic neighborhood,
several miles above the camp ground, and held Mass. On Monday morning
he returned, and came into the camp ground quite drunk. His name was
Oly. He said he would preach for the Methodists for a "Fippeny bit".
He would preach either for them, or against them, he didn't care which.
Being "pretty drunk", the Preachers hustled him off the ground. As
he was getting into his buggy, a common member of the church met him.
The Priest said to him, "Here, I believe all those Methodist Preachers
are uneducated. I don't believe one of them can conjugate a Greek
Verb". He took a pencil out of his pocket, and a piece of paper and
wrote a verse in Greek upon it. "There, said he, "go and give that
verse in Greek to the Preachers, and tell them to translate it."

61

The man fortunately understood Greek, and turned up the paper and translated it, and said to the Priest, I am only a common member, and I can translate your Greek. The Priest gave his horse a cut, and away he went. The man's name is Reuben Meek. He is now Editor of a paper in Bellefonte. Perhaps, he was the only person on the ground that understood Greek. It was a happy bit. In the fall of that year, my plastering comrade, Uriah, went home to go to school, and George Moore moved to Birmingham for the winter only. I remained with him during the winter, and went to school to Daniel Brien, of whom I have formerly spoken, as throwing sulphur down the chimeny when "barred out". Here, in Birmingham, though not a Teacher, I gave my first private lessons on English Grammar to the Rev. Isaac Stratton, who intended to enter the traveling connection of the M. E. Church. He was an excellent; and apt learner; and became a very fine Preacher.

In the Spring of 1834, Mr. Moore moved back again to Mill Hall, and joined partnership with my Uncle Joel Ferree in the plastering business. This was my last summer with George Moore: the time of my apprenticeship being completed. My Uncle was an active man, and did not give us much time to play as we had been accustomed to. He kept us busy at work with his own two apprentices, Adam Gift, and John Robison, who were excellent workmen. He soon had all four of us apprentices out on the mountain top by the week cutting down Hemlock trees; sawing them off lath-length; then clearing them into bolts; and finally splitting the bolts into laths. In those days, all laths for plastering were thus worked out. Sawed laths from the mills were not then thought of. This was an after invention, and a most valuable, profitable, and labor-saving improvement. At night, we found sweet rest in sleeping on a pile of hemlock brush, mantled under a coverlet. This mountain exercise was a fine for making muscle and good blood. The ground was our table-big enough. We had no great variety of provisions on it. In the morning we breakfasted

on bread and, coffee and a cold, boiled "Hug-Jub", (hogs head), as my
Uncle Joel called it. For dinner, we had cofee, bread, and "Hug-Jub".
For supper, we had "Hug-Jub", bread and coffee. We feasted lustily on
these various provisions, for our appetites were voracious and excellent.
We put in a summer of full work; nothing especially transpiring worthy of
record.

My apprenticeship being completed in the fall of this year,
1834, I was, by custom and contract, entitled to a "Freedom Suit", as it
was called. The purchase was made, consisting of rather coarse, brown
cloth. It was soon at the Tailor's; my measure taken; and my impatient
anticipations daily expected. Saturday evening conveyed the intelli-
gence that my new suit was through the Tailor's hands, and ready for my
Sunday apparel. Jubilant, I fled to the shop for my coveted wardrobe.
The Tailor said, "The making of the suit is not paid for, and you cannot
have them. This was an inexpressible mortification to me. It wan my
"Freedom-suit", which I was cherishing to exhibit on Sunday, to-morrow.
"Well, said the Tailor, "The making of the suit is eight dollars; if you
go Moores' security for making them, you can have them." I said, I will:
and he gave them to me. Moore never paid the bill; so that I had the
pleasure of paying it myself. I, afterwards worked as a journeyman for
him, but never got a cent. He, afterwards removed to Hannibal, Missouri,
and gave me an order on a man in Clearfield Co., but the man did not owe
him anything. Sic transit gloria mundi.

Our work for which we contracted for the season being all
completed, we closed up business, as the cold weather was setting in.
The fall was now fast advancing, and the people of Mill Hall began to
think about their winter school. Public schools had not yet been established in Pennsylvania. Schools were sustained by personal subscriptions. Parents subscribed for as many children as they intended to send
to school. The tuition was from one dollar to one dollar and a half for

each pupil, for a quarter, or three months. They applied to me to take
the school. This I refused to do, because I did not deem myself qualified to teach. But they would not accept my refusal, and insisted that
I should take the school. I, therefore, waived my objection, and took
the school. It was in the basement of the Methodist Church. The school
was large, but I succeeded quite beyond my expectations. The Patrons
were will pleased with my success. I taught three months. That was the
accustomed length of time to teach a winter school in those days.

The spring of 1835 having arrived, I again took up the trowel
and hawk, and busily employed myself in the line of plastering.

Charles Callahan, a merchant tailor of Bellefonte, built a
very superior, brick mansion, very costly, and elegant, one of the very
best in the state. The man who did the plain plastering, could not do
the ornamental part of the plastering work. Mr. Callahan, therefore,
employed Isaac Ditsworth of Salone, and formerly from Harrisburg, and a
most superior workman and mechanical genius, to do the ornamental part of
the plastering. He made various patterns and moulds to accomplish this.
Mr. Ditsworth employed John Robison and myself to aid him in this work.
We made fine, beautiful center circles in his parlors for his chande-
liers; ornamental stucco work, and very large, and deep projecting mouldings round the angles in his parlors and rooms. We made all the mouldings out of the purest cream of whitest lime and Plaster Paris. The
finished work was the praise of Mr. Callahan, and the wonder and admiration of the town. This work being completed, and I having no other work
immediately on hand, I decided to go to school a week or two at the
Bellefonte Academy kept by William Hamilton. He was a native of Pine Creek
below Lock Haven. I bought his Algebra, "Bonny Castles" work: it was the
first Algebra I had ever seen. The price was twenty cents. It was my
chief study while I was there. The Algebra was an old English work too
difficult for young beginners. Perhaps there was not then an American

Algebra published. In publishing the old school books, it was no part of the intention of Authors to simplify and make books easy to apprehend. Books for children were written and published for youth the same as for adults. Modern Authors have made a wonderful revolution in this respect. Mr. Hamilton afterwards studied for the Presbyterian ministry, and went West as a missionary.

Having completed by fall work of 1835, I applied to the Directors of Lamar Township for a winter school. When the public Schools of Pennsylvania commenced, 1834, the rude temples of learning were still principally log buildings. Salona, however, could boast over all others of having the best and most substantial school house in the Valley. It was an octagonal, stone structure, admirably adapted to school purposes of that day. For twenty years, at least, this excellent, but too small, noble edifice gathered within it's walls for instruction, the youth of Salona and vicinity. But for it's too limited dimensions, it might have still remained to the present day, firm on it's foundation, faithfully resisting tendencies to decay, and a revered monument perpetuating the memory and educational achievements of the past. It was removed from it's foundation in 1850, and not in 1849, as stated by Prof. M. W. Herr, former County Superintendent, in his school report. The writer taught the last school in it in 1850. On it's site was erected the present, elegant edifice of finer dimensions. Prior to the establishment of the public School System in Pennsylvania 1834, the condition of the State, educationally, was poor indeed. There were 400,000 children of school age in the State that had not been in a school room.

The public schools in Lamar Township (then Center County: Clinton was formed in 1839) commenced in the fall of 1835, and not in 1834, as stated by Prof. Herr, in his report. The writer has a very vivid remembrance of it. He was one of the seven Teachers who opened the first public schools in Lamar Township that year. The Teachers were Samuel Hartman, James Crawford, George Furst, John Brady, James Stevenson,

E. G. Bartram, and J. W. Ferree, the writer.

The Directors assigned the Hamburg or Muckeyville school to me. When Monday morning arrived, I hastened to the scene of my labors, but a certain gentleman, Mr. Reesman, anticipated my coming, and he was also early on the spot when I arrived. He had the windows and door strongly bolted, and ferociously avowing that "no public school Teacher should have admission into the school house". He said, "he was the proprietor of the house and grounds: the school house was on his premises, and he did not believe in the public schools. If things went on in this way, we would have a King next." Being refused, I reported my refusal to the Directors, and they assigned the school on Cedar Run to me, as no Teacher had been elected for that place.

When the above gentleman, however, better understood the public school system, especially the cheapness of it, and that no King came out of it, he became an advocate of the system. James Crawford of Howard, was afterwards eledted to the Hamburg school. He was a local Methodist Preacher, a most excellent man, but not a very profound scholar.

In many places in the State, the public school system, at first, met with violent opposition; chiefly on the ground of taxation. But when those places saw the good fruits of it elsewhere, and it's cheapness; and it's superior advantages over the old system, their opposition ceased, and they generally became it's friends and warm supporters.

This first term of the public schools in Lamar Township was an unusually short one. On the last day of my school, responding to a few vigorous raps on the outside of the school house door, I hailed William Devling from the central part of the Valley, as my guest. He remarked that their school was out, and had not amounted to much, and he wished me to come over and take up a subscription school. He requested me to state my terms of tuition, and he himself would obtain the names

of the Patrons in the neighborhood, favoring and subscribing to the
school. Their Teacher had been Ezra G. Bartram from abroad. I acceded
to his request; gave him my terms, and, good as his word on the next
Monday morning I found the school house well filled with scholars
anxiously awaiting the arrival of the new Teacher.

I boarded at the house of Mr. Devling, and his hospitalities, and that of his Family to me were never surpassed. On the last day
having closed my school, which was a most pleasant one; and settling up
my accounts, I laid my money, on his table, for my term's boarding.
"Here", said he, "put that money in your pocket: I have nothing against
you, if you have nothing against me." Most assuredly, I remarked, I
have nothing against you, if you have nothing against me, thanking him
most heartily for his gift, and the hospitalities of his house. He
added, "only come and teach our school again." He afterwards paid me a
similiar visit, inviting me to teach their school, but previous engage-
ments made else where always prevented me from teaching their school
again. His eldest daughter, Lavina, a young lady of about sixteen years,
then, and a pupil of mine, some years afterward married the Hon. George
Eldred of Mackeyville. Another daughter became the wife of Hon. D. A.
Beckley, Post Master of Bloomsburg, Columbia Co., Pa., and co-editor of
the "Columbia Republican". A third daughter married the Rev. J. R.
Polsgrove of the Central Pennsylvania Methodist E. Conference. At this
writing, this large entire family have passed away except Mrs. Polsgrove.

CHAPTER XXVII

As allusions have been somewhat minutely detailed in the
preceding chapters pertaining to day schools, it might be pertinent to
furnish also a brief reference to the evening Music Schools, or Singing Schools of the Valley. They were merry occasions of sport, great
enjoyment; and profit. Occasionally only, for recreation chiefly, they
were held in summer evenings. But in the winter especially, they were

held in all the school houses of the Valley weekly.

Some one "Master Piece" (Teacher) would assume the over-
sight wholly of the school during the winter, charging a certain "fee"
for each scholar for a quarter of twelve lessons. The "fee" was moderate,
varying from fifty cents to a dollar. Sometimes, at the close of the
school, for amusement and merrymaking, they would pay off the Master or
Teacher wholly in cents. They thought for his valuable services, he was
fully entitled to a large amount of Specie payments. If the snow was
fine and the sleighing good, two or three dozen of young folks would
pile into a large sled, drawn by two spans of horses, well covered with
bells, and flee off for many miles to some other far distant singing
school. We had no lamps in those early days or nights. Neither coal
oil nor coal had yet been discovered. Each scholar took a candle in
his hand, or in his pocket. For a Candlestick during the singing,
"Snuffers" made of a "thumb and finger" were used, to quickly snap off
the top of the wick, or sever the burnt carbon from the flame. It was
found by experience, that it was not good policy to continue the
"snuffers" too long on the wick, as it was said, it was often apt to
generate unexpected troubles, and sometimes lively emotions. All the
musical works, for Vocal music, were published in "Patent notes", or for
a "Slur", were called "buckwheat" notes, because of their forms. Weyth's
musical book was a most excellent one, and was used for a great many years.
It contained very many most excellent pieces of music, and abounded in a
great variety of fine anthems, all of which were sung with great, musical
effect. Such was the almost constant practice and experience of the
voices of these musical schools, that they became very highly cultured
and musical. Their voices on the various parts were very superior.
Though many years have passed since then, I have no hesitancy in saying,
I have never heard better voices: none even so good. I would prefer hearing them now, to any of our modern choirs. I would now walk many miles to
hear such music as I heard sixty years ago.

68

To Salona was accorded the best musical mart in the Valley.
Indeed, it was credited, to be, far and near, the chief storehouse of
music in Central Pennsylvania. It was fitly styled the land of song:
the land of "men-singers", and the land of "women-singers". It's
musical history spans a period of more than sixty years. It has always
kept abreast of the musical times, and held the supremacy without a
rival. Long since it achieved a distinction in the science, that
established it's musical reputation afar. Criticism has never periled
the musical fame of Salona. The musical harmony of cultivated voices
in Salona, has long regaled the senses like gentle breezes through
orange groves; or the subdued echoes sent from soothing hart strings.
The rich, exquisite tones of thrilling anthems in it's schools and churches
have, from times remote enraptured the ear, and seemed like Seraph Voices
from the afar off spheres. The leading Chiefs who have exercised
dominion in this fine Art, have been found principally in the Families
of the Wilsons, Hartmans, and Herrs. They have always been the musical
pioneers and led the van. Our limits will permit us to furnish but few
detailed descriptions of the numerous directors, whose contributions to
the general, musical associations have been most valuable acquisitions.

Samuel Hartman, in former years, was one of Salona's most
successful musical Instructors. He has always been quoted and accounted
as chief among those possessing lowest voice tones. His voice, a rich
basso, was accurate, full and musical. Its deep, powerful tones were
pure, well sustained and greatly admired. It combined a majesty and
sublimity seldom equaled. His instructions were careful, full and thorough.
Uriah Herr, another musical Instructor, for many years stood nobly among
the directors of music in Salona and the Valley. Naturally invested with
a fine musical talent; his voice delicate and rich, he gave great beauty
to his "airs", like tints of harmony on the canvass. His strains were
clear and elegant, and, when he was inspirited by his melodies, his efforts

were grand and masterly. In the schools, sublime, musical compositions
were borne grandly onward, while his voice gave direction and complexion
to the harmony.

In the catalogue of musical Instructors in the schools,
however, who have stood at the helm, and they are many and eminent, it is
no disparagement to the entire roll to say, that Samuel Wilson of Salona,
has always stood at the front leading the van and crowning the list. He
made his first public bow in the vocal Profession in about the year 1830.
His entrance in the musical field, gave a new, fresh impulse; a marked
epoch in church chorals, and the musical schools of the Valleys. His
voice, a rich soprano, controlled with admirable skill; capable of great
tenderness and beauty; replete and inexhaustible; rolled onward with con-
summate mastery. The compass of his voice was about three octaves. There
are few persons in central Pennsylvania, who have not heard the musical
sweetness, power and compass of his voice; or heard the Fame of the exquisite musical richness of his voice that held his audience spell-bound.
Blessed with fine physical strength, and free from a delicate, nervous
organization, he, hence, possessed a calm self-control. In the midst of
a band of vocal choristers, the tones of his voice could always be heard
strongly reaching a height that towered far above all other voices. In
force, enthusiasm and unfaltering execution, he was without a rival.
When in the prime of life, and his sympathies were quickened by the
magnetic power of his voice-tones, his melodies would have done honor to
the musical intellect of Beethoven. Strong in musical expression, his
strains swept athwart his audiences like the rippling of ivory keys of
the piano. All ears were entranced by the torrents of musical elocution
that rolled from his lips. His lyre could touch with finest emphasis the
delicate variations of choromatic passages, and the nice deviations of
accidental sharps and flats. None yet treads in his footsteps. He stood
Master. Had he, in early life, thrown himself upon the public stage, he
would have been the recipient of golden medals at home, and Royalty abroad.

70

We hope this delightful Art, long cultivated with ardor and success in Salona, will never leave its accustomed home and abide elsewhere. May its choral symphonies never descent to a lower level, nor its musical flame be less brilliant. May its musical lights never be extinguished.

CHAPTER XXVIII

Having closed my Spring School of 1836, and having taught several terms in the common schools, successfully as a I thought, still I by no means considered myself competent, or well qualified to teach. I considered my education very limited: only somewhat familiar with the common branches. I always cherished a desire for an extensive education: not that I might be more fully qualified to teach, for I then did not intend to make teaching my Profession. I thought only of the trowel, hawk, and the mortar bed. I desired an education irrespective of any Profession. As no one in the Valley could teach the higher branches, I therefore, decided to go to Allegheny College, located at Meadville, Crawford Co., Pa. Hence I made preparations to be at the College the commencement of the session. I bid "good-bye" to the members of the Family, putting my trunk and its contents in the Stage, leaving my mother in tears, weeping. She always wept when I left home for a long time, and shouted when I returned. I arrived safely and found all things at the College very pleasant. The Faculty was very able and pleasant: all being Preachers: the College being a Methodist one. Dr. Martin Ruter was President, and Jomer J. Clark, D.D. was Vice President, besides several others, and also Subordinate Teachers. I found the students very social. Going to College the first time is quite an epoch in a boy's history. I found a great rivalry between the Literary Societies of the College. When a new student arrives, the students of these societies swarm about him, requesting him to join their society: assigning a score of reasons why he should do so, and a score of reasons why he should not join the other societies.

71

The members of the other Societies are also "playing the same game". This
dishonorable practice among students of all Colleges is not to be commended:
and yet the higher class of upright students are found engaged in it.

This session, I took up Latin, Greek, Algebra and Geometry.
The session Having well nigh absorbed the contents of my pocket book; I
was compelled to bid adieu for the time being, and seek some employment
to replenish my purse. I therefore directed my steps homeward, and was
elected by the School Directors to the school in the East End of Nittany
Valley. This is the school formerly taught by Harvey French, of whom I
have spoken in a preceding chapter.

A rather amusing incident transpired in Mill Hall before I
arrived home. As my name was associated with it, I may summon a little
vanity in detailing it. In my absence at College, a young Doctor of considerable physical magnitude came to Mill Hall, and put out his "shingle".
He was very pompous, and conceited: a great braggadocia. He hailed from
Jersey Shore: having attended school there in an Academy, which gave him
additional "swelled-headism". He carried up in his high "stove pipe" a
problem in Algebra, a puzzle he claimed to have solved in the Academy. He
assumed to be quite scholarly. He took great pride in showing all the
boys, young and old, in shops his problem. He was always at it. No one
in the town, however, understood Algebra. The boys had not much confidence
in it, and would rejoice to see the Doctor taken down a little. They were
on tiptoe when they learned I was coming home from College. They thought
perhaps I might ghrow a shadow on the Doctor's puzzle, which he was ex-
hibiting all summer. The evening I arrived home, the boys had all arranged
to be in a neighbors harness shop, and invite me in. They knew the
Doctor would be there to show his puzzle. I accepted the invitation, and
went over. The shop was crowded. The boys were jubilant: in high spirits.
Boys love sport as I have often said. I assumed to be very grave and sober,

not entering at all in their hilarities. Yet, I saw considerable mudg-
ing and elbow touchings which I pretended not to see or decipher.
Presently the Doctor came in, when the boys were all in a ferment,
anxiously hoping that some mishap or disaster would turn up, unfavorable
to the Doctor's boasted puzzle. The Doctor was introduced to me, and
remarked,"You have been to College, Mr. Ferree", Yes sir, said I. "Did
you study Algebra, said he". A little said I. Said he, "I have an
Algebra problem, a puzzle, I should like you to look at. I worked it out
in the Jersey Shore Academy". The boys saw that things were moving in the
right direction, and were in quiet convulsions. I said, I should like to
see your puzzle, Doctor. The Doctor quickly went up to his "stove pipe"
brought out his problem and gave it to me. The boys were in a ripple-a-
stir. "Go up to the candle and examine it", said the Doctor. The Doctor,
as well as the boys, seemed jubilant, anticipating my approval, looking
scholarly. Doctor, said I, I here discover a great mistake in your
solution, and egregious error, that runs through all the successive, remaining steps of your solution; it annihilates, and makes void, or
destroys your whole work. It makes your solution false. The boys began to
buzz like bees in a hive. "No sir, no sir", said the Doctor, "the Teacher
in the Academy at Jersey Shore said my solution was right". I said, I
don't know anything about the Jersey Shore Teacher, or his qualifications
in Algebra. But you have violated the Law of all Algebras, and Authors
on Algebra. "What's wrong, what's wrong about it?" said the Doctor. Why
said I, you have made the sum of the square roots equal to the square root
of the sum. "They are both alike, they are both alike", screamed the
Doctor. Young Gentleman, said I, give me this blackboard and a piece of
chalk, till I explain. I said, I take the two numbers 16 and 9. The sum
of their square root is 7. But if I add them, and take the square root,
I get only 5, which is the square root of their sum. The Doctor's puzzle
never went up into his "stove pipe" again, nor found it's way to the

at about a half mile from my school house. I had to go through fields
and over fences to make my way to the school house. In this I succeeded
tolerably well, until the deep snows set in. There being no matches in
those days, (except marriage matches) I was compelled to carry a shovel
full of live coals from my boarding place to the school house. This task
was by no means pleasant, especially when the snow was two or three feet
deep, and the big flakes still coming down and promising more, and no
broken path in which to travel. Or when the wind was blowing lustily,
or the rain in plentiful, copious drops seamingly anxious to cool off the
coals on my shovel. The table, too, at my boarding place was not a
feast. It was in harmony with the shovel exercise. For dinner we had a
chunk of boiled pork and potatoes. For supper, what remained after
dinner came back cold. For breakfast, we finished the final dinner
remains. These repititions continued until they became unendurable
(that is by the Teacher). At last, I inquired of my host, what was the
price of boarding. He said, he supposed about two dollars and a half a
week. The Valley price was one dollar and twenty five cents. I "pulled"
up stakes","took out", and secured first class board for one dollar and
twenty five cents. My school was a very pleasant one, and the scholars
improved rapidly. Satisfaction was given, and my services well apprecia-
ted by the Patrons.

This summer (1837) I employed myself in Partnership with my
old apprentice comrade, Uriah, in the plastering business. We plastered
a house at Howard; a church at Beech Creek; besides other work at various
places in the Valley. Our summer's work being completed, and the fall
and cold weather setting in, I was elected by the School Directors to
teach the school in Salona. The school was a very heavy one. I had 125
scholars on hand. I had to summon all my activity and energy to
successfully meet the demand.

74

Most happily, however, I succeeded admirably; was highly commended by the
Directors; and pleased my Patrons. I also had a large night school, in
which I taught English Grammar principally. Having closed my school in
the spring of 1838, I decided to return again to Allegheny College. My
religious convictions being deepened, I judged it wise, and my duty to
attend more earnestly to my religious interests. Rev. John Rhoads, our
preacher, requested me to give him my name for Church Record, which I did.
Since that auspicious hour, I have endeared (alas too feebly) to dedicate
myself more fully to the Lord: and I entertain a blessed hope that,

> "When life shall sink apace,
> And death shall heave in view
> Not fearing or doubting with Christ on my side
> I hope to die shouting, the Lord will provide."

I now began to make preparations to depart for College. My
arrangements being completed, I bid adieu to the Family, took the Stage,
and again leaving my Mother weeping. To me, as well as the Family, these
were occasions of great tenderness. My Mother, especially, was a woman of
wonderful kindness and sympathy. My departure, to her, was almost beyond endurance. In her presence I had to stifle my own feelings, and
suppress my emotions. A Mother's love for her children is unquenchable.
The distance, by Stage, to the College was about 200 miles. When I
arrived at Curvensville, a town on the mountains,I left the Stage for a
day or two, to visit my Uncle William Haslet who lived eight or ten
miles above Curvensville on the river (Susquehanna, West Branch). When
I returned to take the Stage on foot, I had to pass through, and a few
miles beyond the town. Going down a very long steep hill, dense woods
being on each side of the road, the recollection flashed into my mind,
that I was in the regions where Monks lived who murdered Reuben Giles:
which I have described in a previous chapter. My feelings were suddenly
and fearfully wrought up to a high degree, lest a similar incident might
be my fate. When I got to the foot of the hill, a few rods from me, a
hunter suddenly sprant out of the thick woods and stood on the road side.

75

He was dressed chiefly in the costume of wild animals, with a gun on his
shoulder. "There he is", said I, to myself. "I'm a gonor". In a moment
I must determine what's to be done. Shall I stop, or turn and run up the
hill, or pass on? In any position, I cannot escape, for he is too near
me. I decided to go on, tremblingly. I bid him the time of day and he
me. I looked round every few steps to see the bullet coming. But the
hunter crossed the road, and entered the woods. I ascended the hill
"Presto". (quick)

> "In all my ways Thy hand I own,
> Thy ruling Providence I see:
> Assist me still my course to run;
> And still direct my mind to Thee."

I spent another very pleasant session at College. Four
students of us clubbed together, as we called it, and boarded ourselves.
Dr. Homer J. Clark gave us a fine room in the basement of the College
building. The name of the students were William S. Baird from Liberty,
below Lock Haven, Robert Turner from Jersey Shore; James Wilson from
Williamsport, and J. W. Ferree from Mill Hall. We took our turns weekly
in furnishing and preparing the provisions for our table. It is said that
"variety is the **spice** of life". But we did not find the maxim true.
For our tongue detected nothing especially savory in our aromatic sub-
stances, or odor of spices in our "bill of fare". The foot note also states,
however, Rules have their exceptions. The exception, I suppose, was our
category. We boarded, that session, for 40 cents a week each.

When the vacation of 1838 arrived, I remained at the College.
The Trustees of the College employed me to plaster the fourth story of
the main College building. It had never been plastered, or used for any
purpose whatever. I gave it a splendid, white, hard coat finish, it's
polished surface gleaming like glossy marble. When finished, the Trustees
presented the two large rooms to the two Literary Societies: the Allegheny
and the Philo Franklin.

76

The Trustees also put up a Dormitory for boarding students, and gave me the plastering of this building also. Frank Piepoint, a student from Wheeling, Va., also remained here during the vacation, and being "a little short", begged me to give him some work to do, to pay for his board. I put him to nailing on lath. He graduated; went home; studied Law; and was elected the first Governor of Western Virginia. One Saturday morning during the session, he came hastily into my recitation room and said, "here, Ferree, solve this problem in Algebra, for me, I can't get it". I said, Frank, I havn't time, I am writing a composition, and the bell will soon ring. "Here, said he, "I'll finish your composition, and you solve this problem". All right, said I. The following was the closing strain in the composition. "A student by close, continuous application to his studies, will rapidly succeed, and be crowned in his efforts, rising higher, and still higher, until he is sustained by the very sublimity of his elevation".

Besides the above work done in plastering, I did some Plastering for the President, Dr. Homer J. Clark. I taught him how to make the mortar, and he carried it himself on his back. I thought a man of his cloth, education and culture, would not have done so. But in all respects, he was one of the grandest men living, without "airs", or conceit. He was the most thorough man in College in all the Departments. Every student feared his criticisms. I also did some work for the Rev. Ralph Clapp, the stationed Methodist Preacher. Towards the close of vacation, a plasterer came down from Rockford, a town 8 miles from Meadville, wanting a plasterer to run a center piece in a new church for a chandelier. He could find no one to do it. Someone directed him to me. I gladly did it for the fellow. By these various employments, I gathered funds to continue in College. Hence I entered the fall session of 1838. After the holidays a school director from Sagertown, a Village six miles from Meadville, came to Meadville in search of a School Teacher. Not finding any in

town, he came up to the College in pursuit of one. The students pointed
me out as having taught. He came to me and said, "we have dismissed our
teacher, and have yet fifty dollars of school money still remaining in
the Treasury: and we want a teacher for two months". I said, I will take
the school. On Monday morning I took my books in Latin, Greek, Algebra,
and Geometry, Logic and Rhetoric, intending, if possible, to keep up with
my classes in College. When I entered the school room, I found ninety
scholars waiting my arrival, and ready to greet me. I organized and proceeded pleasantly after a brief address which I had always been accustomed
to give my schools. I was informed on every hand, that there was a certain
young fellow, called ""Bil", who was an "out-law" every where, and would
give me trouble. No teacher had ever tamed, or conquered him, or brought
him to terms. He was a bound boy and lived in the country with a farmer,
who was accustomed to apply the lash to him terribly almost every day.
It was said, the boy, "Bil's" back had long since lost it's tenderness, and
had the induration, or solidity of a shark's skin. He smiled only at
cart whips well laid on. The reports gave me some uneasiness. These
statements assured me, in case of trouble with him, the rod was useless.
It was said, he will keep straight a day or two in school, and then he
will make a break to see what sort of stuff the new Teacher is made of.
And I found it so. The scholars all the while keeping their eyes on "Bil",
expecting a collision with the Teacher. Finally "Bil" achieved a piece
of misconduct in the presence of the school, which for the sake of good
discipline, it would not do to let pass unnoticed, though it was his first.
I called him up immediately to my desk; he bolted up with a supremacy,
and arrogant majesty. Everybody called him "Bil". I changed it, and
gave him a new name, calling him William. It pleased him. After some
little pause, keeping him standing, I said in a soft, mellow tone,

78

"How old are you William?

"Sixteen years":he answered.

Do you live in the town?

"No sir: I live in the country".

Do you live far away?

"About a mile".

How long have you been going to school?

"Every winter".

Do you think an Education is a good thing?

"Yes sir".

Do you think people can get along well without it?

"No sir.

Do you find old people going to school, or young people?

"young people."

Can old people learn as well as young people?

"No sir".

Do you wish to have a good education, William?

"Yes sir."

Do you know that school days quickly pass away?

"Yes sir."

Do you not know, William, that to be honored by the people, and trusted, and loved, and successful in life, we must be intelligent, and wise, and good?

"Yes sir."

Is your Father living, William?"

"No sir; he's dead".

Is your Mother living?

"No sir; she's dead too."

Did you love your Mother?

"Yes sir."

79

When you were a little boy, did your Mother teach you
little hymns to sing, and to pray? His lips quivered;
he bowed his head, and said,

"Yes sir."

Were you at home when your Mother died?

"Yes sir."

Were you in the house?

"Yes sir."

Were you in her room?

"Yes sir."

Did she say anything to her William when she was dying?
The tears streamed down from his eyes, and he sobbed aloud,
but could not answer.

Did she wish you to be good and meet her in Heaven?

"Yes sir".

(Handkerchiefs went up to many eyes in the school room)

Did you promise her you would?

"Yes sir."

And are you keeping your promise?

He did not respond.

I said, be a good boy, William, and the people will love you,
and God will love you, and take care of you: and when you die, He will
send His angels down to take you up to Heaven, and there to see your
Mother, and let her know that you kept your promise. I never afterward
had occasion to speak even to "Bil" in school. He was among the very best
scholars I had. Kindness, tenderness, and sympathy will sometimes achieve
wonders and success, when physical punishment will not. My two months
school being very successfully and satisfactorily closed in Sagertown, I
returned to College and re-entered my classes.

80

In the spring and summer session, I boarded with the President,
Dr. Homer J. Clark. When the session closed in July 1839, my purse being
well nigh exhausted, I returned home hoping to replenish it in some way.
I was elected by the Directors to the school above Salona, near the old
Methodist Church (now removed). I objected to the school, as it was one
of only two months: the school funds being mostly taken to build the
new school in which I was to teach. George Hartman, however, being the
chief school Director there, and having control of the house, promised me
a large subscription school after my two months had expired. He said it
would furnish me more money than three months more of public school. I
therefore acceded to his request and plan. When the last day (Saturday)
of the two months had expired, in violation of his contract with me, he
came into the school house, and not saying a word to me, announced to the
school that his son Albert would take up a school there, beginning on the
following Monday morning. Two or three scholars only came out. The people
were indignant. His son was not qualified to teach. After two or three
days, he gave it up. Thus, I was cheated out of a winter school mostly,
and was unable to return to College on account of funds. Perhaps I could
have legally prosecuted him for a violation of contract.

The Spring of 1840 opening, Mr. Saul McCormick, a merchant
and man of influence in Mill Hall, requested me to take up a school there.
I told him that Mr. Black had just commenced a school, and was occupying
the school house. He said, "Mr. Black must get out of that: he is not
qualified to teach, if you will agree to teach, I'll put him out, and give
you the key of the school house." I said, I do not wish to be responsible
for his removal. "I'll see to that", said he. I said if the house was
vacant, I would teach. "Very well", said he, it will be vacated. I
pitied Mr. Black, for he was a nice man and lame. The key was demanded,
and the house made ready for me, and I opened a large school. I taught
through the summer, and continued the school through the winter.

81

In the spring of 1841, I made preparations to build a house
in Mill Hall, to be occupied by my Father. I had previously purchased a
lot from Aunt Barnet in Lancaster City, through George Herr's son, as
her agent. The foundation was dug; the cellar was walled; and the axe
was on my shoulder going to the mountains about Mill Hall to fell trees
for my lumber. But a certain man, named Nathan Harvey, hailed me on my
mountain journey, and laid an embargo upon my jubilant intentions, which
brought my plans to a "stand still": he "claimed the timber on the
mountains, and forbid anyone from molesting it". This was a great dis-
appointment and "draw-back" to me, for my funds were very limited, and I
was unable to purchase the lumber I wanted for my house. I was quite
"down in the mouth", and discouraged, in being ordered away from the
mountain slopes.

To obtain information as to Mr. Harvey's pretended claim to
the mountains, I went up to the Valley and consulted Joseph Quay about it.
Joseph was a practical Surveyor. He had surveyed nearly all the lands in
the country, and seemed to know almost every stake in it. Mr Quay was a
man of great influence: correct, honest, truthful, brave, courageous,
upright. No one dared to question any statement he made. His word was
Law in the Courts, and every where else. How valuable such a man is in
a community. I knew him well. As I went along on the road almost tearfully on my errand to see him in my troubles, I thought on the way, if
Joseph can only favor, or aid me in any way, what a blessing it will be
to me. Otherwise, all my summer plans and calculations for building
my house will be frustrated. How unpleasant it is to be cherishing doubt
and uncertainty in important things in our concerns, or in which we are
deeply interested. Joseph was always very friendly to me. He once saw a
piece of my writing, or penmanship, and said, "Wesley, throw away your
trowel, hawk, mortar bed, and all your plastering tools. "A young man
that can play that kind of a pen, is cut out for a higher Profession." I

timber question, and how Nathan had ousted me off the mountain, claiming the mountains as his own. "The rascal", said he. "He does not legally own a bush on the mountains, and never did. He has always made the people believe the mountains were his. He has stripped most of the best timber off them, sawed it, and sold it, when he could not claim a stick of it. They are public unseated lands, belonging to nobody. Go Wesley, take all the timber you want: every stick of it if you want it. If Nathan disturbs you again, I'll cool him down." Nathan heard that I had seen Joseph. He never said another word about it. I went home jumping high as a stump, jubilant, that to me was bequeathed a mountain. Soon again the axe was on my shoulder and among the trees loud sounding,

Redoubling strokes on strokes
On all sides hurling down pines and oaks.

The house work was kindled up again, and things went on cheerily. The trees were felled, and severed from their trunks; hand-spiked down the mountain into the creek; floated to the saw mill; then sawed; and put into a canoe; and my strength manifested in conveying away scores of boat loads some distance up the creek to the intended residence. These boat excursions were substitutes for wagons, and wagon prices. The boat trips tested the muscles. My Father and I finished the house very neatly, and lived in it fifteen years.

The fall approaching, I was again elected by the Valley Directors to the Cedar Run School. I boarded at Aunt Harriet Millers on the mountain side: residence of the late Breasler Herr. The spring opening, I again worked at my trade with Uriah, during the summer:1842.

In the fall of 1842, I was elected by the Mill Hall Directors to their school. On January 5th, 1843, I was married to Miss Frances Ann Herr, who had lived most of her life in Lancaster City with her Aunt Charlotte Barnett. Her parents, however, lived in Nittany Valley. Her Aunt Barnett presented her a beautiful Mahogany Bureau, and beautiful, rich dishes of great value. She was a christian Lady, good, noble, brave,

and true. We occupied a part of the house we built. The following
summer, (1843) I worked some at my trade, and also assisted my Father
in painting. In the fall I was elected to teach the school again above
Salona, which I had taught before.

In the summer I was again at my trade: 1844. I was tired,
and discouraged in teaching so long in the common schools at such low
prices. About twenty five dollars a month was regarded as a high price.
I decided to go South for higher prices.

I might have said above, that a certain Weather Prophet, or
rather historian, of Lock Haven, publishing the winters of past years,
said "that closing winter 1842, and beginning of 1843, was a very open
winter: that all the ice on the river was gone before and after the
holidays." I made void his statement in his Newspaper, that in the winter
referred to, I knew a Wedding Party (my own) that crossed the river on
ice, in sleighs, Jan. 5th, 1843.

I now began to make preparations to go South. In September
therefore, leaving my wife at home, and being accompanied by Mr. Albert
Hartman, also a teacher, we began our journey by canal boat to Pittsburg.
Here we took a Steamboat for the whole length of the Ohio River, 1000 miles.
Our voyage down the River was slow on account of the very low water.
We spent two or three weeks on it. When we reached the Mississippi River
we went down by SteamBoat 250 miles further to Memphis, Tennessee. Here
we left the boat, and struck out for schools. After inquiring very
generally for vacant schools in the city, and finding none, we canvassed
the vicinity, but all in vain. I was getting a little "down in the mouth",
and discouraged: for we were far from home, and our purses light. Going
still a little further out, and still making constant inquiries about
schools, nothing but discouragement met us at every step. Nothing promising was in prospect. If we returned homeward our purses would refuse to
carry us there. We were in a dilemma we did not anticipate.

84

Our imaginations were not sufficiently fruitful to devise means to
emerge from our troubles. "We were at our wits end." Finally, we saw
in the distance, a rather old man coming on the road meeting us, lean-
ing on his staff. I said, we will inquire of him. When he came up we
spoke to him: we paused. I said, do you know of any vacancy for a school
about here?   "Are you a Teacher"? said he

                I said, I try to teach sometimes.

                "Where are you from Sir"? said he.

                I said, I am from the North.

            "Ah! I am from the North myself:said he

            "What State are you from, sir?"

        I said, I am from Pennsylvania.

            "Why", said he, "I am from Pennsylvania."

        "What County are you from Sir", said he

            I said, now Clinton County; but formerly Center County.

            "Why sir, Center County is my Native County, said he".

            "What part of Center do you hail from"? said he.

        I said, from a town called Mill Hall.

            "Mill Hall, why I was born within a stones throw of Mill
Hall." "A School, a School", said he. Yes: we want a Teacher. We have
been talking about building a new school house. We'll now get right at it:
and you'll be our Teacher." O! my dear Sir, said I: I am on the wing,
and can't wait on building a school house. "Well, said he, "your salary
will begin tomorrow." Allright, said I. Light came suddenly and satisfactorily..My comrade, Albert went on a little farther and also obtained a
school. I went home with the gentleman, Mr. Glen, and the next morning
he put me on the saddle, and we rode round to see a number of the patrons,
he showing my College Recommendations: all seemed jubilant. They went
at the house, and in two weeks I was in it, most happily at work. They said
I was a "Steam Engine". But I wasn't. My companion, Alber, taught a while;

became discouraged; closed his school; went home; leaving me there. I
taught the year out, and at the close of the school had a fine, credit-
able examination. They were all delighted. Every body seemed to be out
at the examination. I gave the scholars and citizens my Farewell
Address; shook hands with all of them. They all wept; and I shared tears
with them. I left the scenes where I spent so many happy days, leaving
them all still lingering there, and all their eyes gazing after me,
until far away, I vanished from their sight. I repaired to my boarding
place, and completed my preparations for departure the next morning.
They were all exceedingly anxious for me to return and continue the
school: they could not give me up. But I could not promise them. I was
too far away from home. The next morning my eyes were anxiously turned
homeward. I was soon on the Steamboat gliding up the Mississippi. When
going up the Ohio River, below Cincinatti, one evening after tea, the
Captain and I were promonading on the hurricane (upper) deck. I said,
Captain, how long have you followed the River? "Just thirteen years",
said he. I said, have you ever met with an accident? "Never one", said
he. The words had scarcely dropped from his lips, until the Steamboat struck a rock in the bed of the River, and was tearing the plank off
the bottom of the boat. The water was rushing in; and the boat began to
rock like a cradle. The Captain called th the helmsman to make for the
shore. The passengers screamed and ran in every direction. The bow of
the boat struck the shore, plowing into the sand, while the hinder part
of the boat went down ten or fifteen feet in the River and filled with
water. The boat lay at an angle of about 45 degrees. It was with
difficulty the boat dragged off the rock. It nearly stopped in it's
movement. If it had, the boat would have fallen over and filled with water
and sunk. The passengers, doubtless would have been drowned. It was a
Providential deliverence. We remained on it during the night. The next
morning, another Steamboat following us, the Captain arranged to put the

passengers on it, paying our fare to Pittsburg: as we previously paid
him. I arrived home safely with gold enough in my purse to pay for my
lot, and all indebtedness, leaving more in the bottom.

In the fall and winter of 1845, I was elected by the School
Directors to the Mill Hall School. My school closing in the spring, I
employed myself at my trade in the summer of 1846. This closed up my
plastering finally. I worked no more at it afterwards.

I now decided to return to the South to teach; but to go to
some Eastern Atlantic State nearer home, and take my wife with me. We
therefore left home in September 1846, bidding again Good-Bye, tearfully,
to the family we left at home. We went by Canal boat and cars to Baltimore. No Railroad then up along the Susquehanna. The Canal Packet ran
from Lock Haven to Philadelphia. The Railroad was finished in the fall
of 1855.

In Baltimore I met an old Methodist Preacher who used to
preach up on our circuit and knew me. His name was Isaac Collins. He
said, "why Ferree, where are you going?" Down South to teach, said I.
Said he, "dont you say "nigger" down there." It was before the War when
slavery ran high. I said, I'm not going for "niggers": that's not my
business. We spent about a week in Baltimore among friends, and then took
the Steamer "Georgia" on the Chesapeake Bay for Norfolk, Va., a distance
of about 200 miles. We left Baltimore at   o'clock, P.M., and arrived in
Norfolk at day light the next morning. In Portsmouth, a large town
opposite Norfolk, we found they were about starting the public schools for
the first time. I reported myself to the Trustees, and they were exceedingly anxious that I should stop on my journey, and take one of their
schools. They would give me a salary of $500. a year. I concluded to
accept. I paused several weeks waiting for the opening of their schools,
but they were so tardy, I got tired waiting on them. I became acquainted
with a Methodist Preacher, Rev. Vernon Eskridge, who was a School Director

in the vicinity. He was anxious for me to take their school. They
would give me $300. out of the school Treasury, and the citizens would
make up a large extra purse besides. So that I would make about as much
as in the town school. I was uneasy in losing time, and decided to delay
no longer, but take the Vicinity School. The town Trustees were mortified
in having lost me. They said, we will keep a place for you, and demand you
when we begin. You must then resign there. But I was pleased where I was,
and boarding was less than in town, so I decided not to change, but
remain where I was. I continued teaching here three years in succession,
and intended to continue. But when we went home in vacation, we found my
sister Jane in very poor health, not expecting to live through the year.
She was, therefore, very unwilling for us to return that year. We
acceded to her request, and remained. That fall, 1849, and the following
winter and summer, I took a school in Salona. My sister died April 2, 1850.
That was the last public school I taught in Pennsylvania. That fall we
again returned to Virginia to my old school. I spent all my years most
pleasantly here, my wife assisting me. The school improved rapidly, and
crowned all other schools. A few weeks before the closing, or vacation of
this year, I received a letter from the Secretary of the Board of Trustees
of an Academy, about five miles from there. The contents of the letter
stated, that the Board of Trustees had elected me as Principal of their
Academy. I must explain this circumstance a little. About one hundred
years previous to the time I received their letter, and Englishman by the
name of Yates came to that part of Virginia, and settled there, remaining
there for life. He acquired a large amount of property. He never married.
In his will, he bequeathed all his property to founding two Academies there,
about six miles apart. The Annual income of his estate was to erect the
Academies (if necessary); pay the salaries of the Teachers, and furnish all
the Stationery for all the pupils within certain limits or boundaries
prescribed by the Will. The income also purchased all the Philosophical,

Chemical, Astronomical, and Mathematical apparatus. Every outfit in
completness was furnished without exception. The citizens there, had
never paid any tuition or any school expense whatever.

The Will directed, that when a Teacher was wanted for either
Academy, at any time, the Trustees must advertise several weeks in the
newspapers, for applicants, and then the applicants were to be examined
by a learned committee, and if approved, then elected by the Trustees.
In my case, they neither advertised nor examined me. They leaped over
all the conditions of the Will, and elected me without my consent or
even knowledge. My Patrons were wonderfully grieved over this incident.
They advised me not to accept my election. They said they were cut up in
parties, and were a discordant element: and I would find it unpleasant
to live among them. They were always quarreling with their Teachers and
dismissing them. They had expelled three Teachers this year: and one of
them, the last one, was a graduate of Yale College. While here it was
quiet and peaceful. I, too, was very much attached to my school, and
would leave it very reluctantly, after teaching it four years. I confess,
too these reports were not very savory. I, therefore, did not favorably
answer their letter of election. They wrote to me again saying, "if you
cannot decide now to come, do not decide not to come." I did not decide
either way before I left for home in vacation. There was but one thing
inducing me to accept favorably: and that was, they gave me $400. more
salary than where I was teaching. I determined that if I should accept,
and find the reports true about their jarrings and dissensions, and they
were keeping them up, and annoying me, I would resign. I would not
endure it. My continuance would turn upon this pivot. They wrote me a
number of letters in vacation at my home, still strongly urging me to
accept my election. Finally, I summoned courage and wrote that I would
accept my election. It was an inexpressible mortification to my Patrons
and Scholars. Such was the high estimate (quite too high) the Scholars

and Patrons had in me, that my successor there could do nothing with the school, and resigned.

My home vacation being about expired, I made preparations to depart to my new charge. I was cherishing some little timidity. When we arrived there, I found all the reports true, but with party differences I had nothing to do. The scholars were also sharing, and taking sides in their discords. I would not hear or identify myself with either. I coveted no desire to continue troubles. I came only to teach, and, if possible, push things vigorously, and with energy in the right directions. Soon all their variations vanished away, and peace, harmony, and good will prevailed every where and between all parties. There was not a jar the two years we were there.

While the above strifes and vexations had previously marred the school, the other Academy had peace. All the wealthy families and better citizens withdrew their patronage, and sent to the peaceful Academy, where they had qualified Teachers. That Academy had a certain Mr. Glen as it's head. His fame was far and wide. He overshadowed all the country. He was drawing pupils from every where. It was all, "Mr. Glen"; "Mr. Glen", over the country. I became alarmed. I said to myself, if Mr. Glen is really sailing on such a high tide, as the people represent, I'll surely go down in the grough of the sea. He'll have all my school away from me. This will never do. I must wake up, put on spurs, or I'll be a "gonor", He'll ruin me, if things go on this way. I determined to set my face to recover things: to make an effort to reinstatement. My efforts caused a pause in going "Glenward". The tide now began to ebb the other way. The scholars that left and went to Glen, began to come back, and continued to flow from Mr. Glen to me, until I emptied him of all the scholars he had drawn away. Even the Trustees in his own limits left him, and sent their scholars to me, although the distance was much further away. The "banner" of Mr. Glen no longer floated truumphantly in the breeze. He became

mortified and discouraged that he had so fallen in public estimation, and
resigned, although he had been teaching there for years. His brilliant
feathers were plucked.

Sic transit gloria mundi.

The school year was a most prosperous one. As the school
year was approaching a close, and vacation coming on, the Trustees began
to make preparations for my examinations. They announced a meeting for the
citizens. They proposed to furnish a public dinner for all the attend-
ing citizens. One said, I will furnish dinner for 75. Another said I will
furnish for 50. Another for 40, and 30, and 20, and 60, and so on.
They dug two parallel trenches or ditches, about 40 or 50 yards long;
two or three feet deep; and two feet wide, and put in them a large
quantity of oak wood-cord like. Then they put up two large, canvass awnings for roofs, as long as the ditches, with tables and seats under them.
I knew from the preparations they were making, that my large school house
would not hold the crowd they were expecting. I decided, therefore, to
hold my examinations out doors. The Trustees had invested me with power
to get anything I wanted for the school, asking no questions of anyone.
So I had a platform laid in front and joining the building; it's breadth
being about ten feet, and covered with carpet and seated. Above the
platform, and the length of the building, was a canvass awning that extended back 60 or 70 feet, and seats under it. I had a black board made
as long as the house and placed above the platform. It was made to fold
up on hinges, after the manner of a rule. All surroundings looked like
business. Work was indicated. Things were to buzz. So they did. The
people were charmed. "They never saw the like": so they said: and no
doubt but they told the truth. "It was something new under the sun."
When the day of examinations arrived, young and old were attired in their
best, and early on the grounds. The commencing hour for exercises found
all the pupils beautifully apparalled and seated on the Platform. While

the examinations were goin grandly forward, the provision hosts were looking after their tables in the physical interests of their guests, while the
cooks with deep ditches of live coals, had suspended, above the fiery
bed, roasting, prepared chickens, turkeys, ducks, geese, pigs, sheep,
hogs, opossums, and oxen in fore quarters, and hind quarters, familiarly
called. Southern people love meats.

The following Pages are read by themselves.
Dates and places where I have taught school.   J.W.F.

1833	I taught Rev. Isaac Stratton Kirkham's Eng. Gramm., Birmingham, Pa.
1834	In Mill Hall, In basement of M.E. Church, By Subscription.
1835	At Cedar Run, First Public School: in spring, I taught in Valley.
1836	East End of Nittany Valley.
1837	In Salona, also large class in Eng. Gram. Night School, New System.
1838	In Sagerstown, Crawford Co.; 6 miles from Meadville. Student.
1839	Near Salona: Present residence of Uriah Herr Esq.
1840	In Mill Hall: Summer and Winter.
1841	At Cedar Run: Near the residence of the late Bressler Herr.
1842	In Mill Hall
1843	Near Salona: Present residence of Uriah Herr Esq.
1844	At Sandy Springs, Fayette Co., Tennessee
1845	In Mill Hall
1846	Near Portsmouth, Virginia: 200 miles south of Baltimore.
1847	" " " "
1848	" " " "
1849	In Salona: also in the summer of 1850.
1850	Near Portsmouth: Virginia.
1851	Elected by Trustees to Yates Academy.
1852	" " " "
1853	Elected to higher Math & Nat. Sci., in Dickinson Sem., Williamsport,Pa
1854	" " " "
1855	" " " "
1856	" " " "
1857	" " " "
1858	" " " "
1859	" " " "
1860	" " " "
1861	" " " "
1862	" " " "
1863	" " " "
1864	" " " "
1865	" " " "
1866	" " " "
1867	Established an Institute in Williamsport, for Ladies and Gentlemen.
1868	Elected to higher Math. and Nat. Sci. in Bloomsburg State Normal
1869	" " " "School.
1870	" " " "
1871	" " " "
1872	" " " "
1873	" " " "
1874	" " " "
1875	" " " "
1876	" " " "
1877	" " " "

92

Continued:
1878   Elected to higher Math. & Nat. Sci. in Bloomsburg State Normal
1879   "   "   "   School.
1880   "   "   "   "
1881   "   "   "   "
1882   "   "   "   "
1883   "   "   "   "
1884   "   "   "   "
1885   "   "   "   "
1886   "   "   "   "
1887   "   "   "   "
1888   "   "   "   "

Let no one laugh, or smile at the prodigious columns, or rows of figures on the preceding pages, indication my successive school teaching days or years. They surprise us or startle us a little. I have passed safely and unhurt through them all, not receiving even a scar. Doubtless, however, many a luckless weight has in memory, numerous incidents, some perhaps a little unsavory, while others cherish delightful things. The Teacher, as well as the pupil, or student, has had his share of delights, and occasionally, wants of pleasantry in them. We delight to hope, however, that both Teacher and pupil have been profited. I derive pleasure in the reflection that a kind Providence assigned me my Profession: bent my directions, and pointed out to me the localities of my life-work; blessed me in it, and approved my well intended, intellectual, moral, and religious instructions. While my Profession aimed chiefly to cultivate the intellect, yet, I always cherished a restless desire to impress moral convictions, and divine things, upon the minds and hearts of students. The natural sciences especially, afford ample fields for illustrating the divine attributes, and leading the mind "from Nature up to Natures God".

In the vacation of 1855, my wife and myself took a trip to the West. We first visited her sister Mrs. Charlotte Moore, in Hannibal, Missouri. She was there taken suddenly with the bilious Fever: not being sick much more than a week, until she died. I brought her home in a metallic coffin. She was buried at Salona. My grief could scarcely be endured. Dr. Bowman went to Salona and preached her funeral sermon.

93

He also preached her funeral sermon at Williamsport. His text was,
Rev. 14th Chapter, and 13th verse, "Write Blessed are the dead which
die in the Lord from henceforth: yea, saith the Spirit, that they may
rest from their labors; and their works do follow them. The following
obituary notice of her was written by Mis Calista Clarke, then
Preceptress at the Seminary, now Mrs. McCabe, wife of Prof. L. McCabe
at the Ohio Wesleyan University.

Aug. 13th in Hannibal, Mo., Mrs. Frances Ann Ferree, wife
of J. W. Ferree, A.M., of Dickinson Seminary, Williamsport,
Pa., aged 34. Surrounded from childhood by influences favor-
able to piety, she experienced a change of heart fifteen
years ago at a Camp Meeting near Salona,Pa, and united with
the M. E. Church. From that time her christian course was
one of undeviating consistency. She was clear and decided
in her religious views; uniform in the performance of duty
and attendance on the means of grace. The Bible was em-
phatically her Book: she read it through once every year
after her conversion. The last two years, as the wife of a
Teacher, she was closely connected with our Seminary; and
during that time, her remarkable practicability and kindness
of heart were displayed in her unremitting attention to those
who surrounded her, often ministering with her own hands to
their comfort. These with her uniform cheerfulness and
affectionate words of encouragement, endeared her to many
young hearts, the pleasantness of whose home in our halls
she so materially promoted. She left with her husband to
visit their relatives in various parts of the West, and
while with her sister was attacked with the bilious fever,
and after an illness of two weeks sank unexpectedly in the
arms of death. During her sickness, she spoke freely of

her religious enjoyments and Heavenly prospects, expressing her
gratitude for the goodness of God; her love to Christ; and her
desire for her Heavenly home. Her countenance brightening up, she
said, "I feel so happy: the Lord is so good to me." And again
"I love Jesus, and I will wait till Jesus comes." When dying, at
her husband's request she endeavored to raise her cold hand in
token of victory. Her happy spirit soon after took it's flight
to a world of glory.

On May 9th, 1860, I was married to Miss Diana Justine Elliott of
Canton, Bradford Co., daughter of Schuyler Elliott esq.

COPY OF LETTER

WRITTEN

TO

IRVIN FERREE, MACKEYVILLE, PENNA.

FROM

J. W. FERREE, PAYNESVILLE

MINNESOTA

                                        Paynesville, Apr. 4, 1894

Very Dear Irvin:

     Our letters, like angel visits, are few and far between,
yet we think of you often, and it is a wonder we don't write
more frequently. I see you have a rail-road through Mackeyville
which must stir you up considerably. They are a great insti-
tution. They have brought us to the far West. Without them,
I suppose we would still be East of the mountains, as we say.
We (Annie and I) expect to go back again on them, next fall, to
visit our old native state and scenes in Clinton County. It will
be delightful to see you all again. It will be 6 years next
summer since we left you. The time seems long and short. The
years fly round quickly. They will soon transport us to the
"Shining Shore." May we be ready.

     We are well. This side of the holidays, I was confined to
my bed 5 weeks, with pneumonia, or inflamination of the lungs.
It requires great care and caution to live in this Minnesota
climate, especially in the spring, fall, and winter. The
weather is very changeable with numerous heavy winds. We can
have several kinds of climate in a day.. One great advantage is
the air is pure and bracing. My physician thinks this climate
is too severe for my lungs. If so, I will have to drop down a
little further south. I will try it, I think, next winter. How
would Salona or Mackeyville do? My physician thinks that even
central Pennsylvania is a little too far north for me in the winter
time. I will have to see about it.

     We make ice here three or four feet thick on our lakes. That
beats Mackeyville. Our snows are very light and dry. We cannot
make snow balls here. We might as well try to make balls out of
dry sand. It is too cold here for fruit trees. I have not seen
an apple tree or peach tree since I have been in Minnesota. I
like peaches, but seldom touch them in the markets. Coming from
the South, they are generally stale and soiled, and have lost
their freshness and flavor. I should like to see a peach tree,
with something on it. We have two garden lots. Last year we had
a large patch of tomattoes, but the frost struck them, and we
lost bushels of them. We had about one meal off them.

     A very heavy hail storm ruined almost the whole of our crops.
Milton got about 60 bushels of wheat off a farm of 200 acres.
This wheat was 50¢ a bushel. Joel got a little more than that.

     Simpson is still in Minneapolis in his Law business. He
is doing well. George (the Doctor) has a large medical practice.
He has put even the other doctors here at rest. Charlie teaches.
He also is doing well. Annies' health is good, but she wearies
under the burdens of house-keeping. I was sorry to learn of the
death of Hon. George Eldred. I knew him well when he lived in
Mill Hall. He taught school there, when I was building my house,
where your grand-pa and grand-ma lived so long - 15 years. Annie
and I were up at your Fathers last fall. Joel is not in very
good health. Last year was a bad year for their crops. The summer
was dry.

They are great fellows to catch wild geese in wild geese
seasons. We lived on them a week there, and brought 2 big
fellows home with us. Our soup dishes were kept full a long time,
with goose products. But, we have eaten them all up, and are
ready for more.

Remember us to Rev. W. H. Geese. I am glad you have him
back again this year with you. Our love to you all. Write soon.

Yours affectionately,

J. H. Harris
Payneeville
Stearns Co.
Minnesota